Will to Survive
Love in the Line of Duty

TO: PATRICIA

M. LEANN

WITH LOVE!

M. LEANN

Will to Survive

Love in the Line of Duty

COPYRIGHT © 2016 M. Leann. All Rights Reserved.

No part of this publication may be reproduced, distributed, or transmitted in any form or by any means, including photocopying, recording, or other electronic or mechanical methods, without the prior written permission of the author, except in the case of brief quotations embodied in critical reviews and certain other noncommercial uses permitted by copyright law.

ISBN 978-0-9982727-0-2 Digital Edition (Kindle)
ISBN 978-0-9982727-1-9 Digital Edition (ePub)
ISBN 978-0-9982727-2-6 Print Edition

M. Leann Publishing
MLeann562@gmail.com
www.facebook.com/MLeann562

DEDICATION

In memory of those that gave all
and in honor of those that still serve.

CHAPTER ONE

"BOY-200, 562. I'VE GOT A possible signal 88, am code 3 near Marigold on the 15 southbound."

David Langley cringed and turned down the volume on his blaring radio. Sighing, he steered his truck onto the highway. He would be passing right by the officer on his drive home.

"562 copy."

Langley's eyes were burning. He couldn't wait to get a hot shower and a couple hours sleep. He'd worked far too late on his reports, tying up the loose ends for his team. It was nearly four thirty in the morning and he had to be back at the station by eleven.

"Boy-200, 562. Signal 88, white male, 37, told me he has a suspended license and warrant. Is 574 available for back up?"

"Negative, 562. 574 is 10-6."

"10-4. Male is out of vehicle, any units available?"

Langley could sense the sudden adrenaline spike in the officer's voice. Although exhausted, Langley didn't hesitate; he picked up the radio and put it to his shoulder.

"562, this is Victor 7."

There was a pause after Langley's transmission.

"Go Victor 7."

"Am 2 minutes away from your 20."

"10-4, Victor 7. Hurry."

Damn!

Langley pressed down on the gas pedal and nudged his holster with his elbow. His service pistol was snuggled up against his rib cage and he could feel the badge pressing through his pants pocket. Taking a deep breath, he rolled back his muscled shoulders and cracked his knuckles against the steering wheel. The shower could wait.

He saw the whirling lights of Officer Woods' patrol car and pulled his truck as far onto the shoulder as possible so he wouldn't block the cruiser's red & blue lights from traffic.

Langley smoothly stepped from his vehicle, his muscular frame unfolding lithely as he jogged towards the police cruiser, boots thudding on the asphalt.

"Woods! It's Langley!" He called out, not wanting to spook the cop. As Langley stepped in front of the spotlights, he swore.

Officer Woods was wrapped up in a bear hug with the drunken driver; they were both cursing and throwing punches, slamming each other onto the trunk of the drunken man's car.

Langley dove in, matching the six-foot-tall suspect in size. Woods was a good foot shorter and was no match physically for the drunkard. Langley grabbed a swinging arm and ratcheted it behind the drunken man's back but couldn't defend against the responding blow from a ham-sized left fist.

"Jesus!" Woods yelled, blocking a groin-aimed kick as he fumbled with his belt.

"No pepper spray!" Langley growled, slamming a knee into the drunkard's stomach. He doubled over and Langley took the opportunity to get a leg behind the man. A shove from Langley's solid shoulder sent the hulking drunk flailing backwards onto the dirt shoulder.

"Taser taser taser!" Woods yelled. Langley retreated hastily as Woods darted onto the shoulder to be in better range of the suspect. The familiar sound of the deployed taser set Langley's hair on end and he heard it make contact when the drunken man howled; he knew they would get no more real resistance from the boozer. The five second ride of the taser still hadn't stopped when Langley felt a tingling at the base of his neck. He glanced over his shoulder.

"Holy—"

But the abrupt squealing of brakes washed out his words. Langley barely had time to jump sideways before the speeding, skidding SUV slammed into the back of Woods' patrol car.

The morning exploded around Langley. His jump saved him from going under the patrol car; instead, his legs bounced off the push bumper and launched his lower body forward, which allowed his torso and head to collide solidly with the patrol car's windshield.

He felt the glass crack and give beneath him, then was immediately catapulted forward as the momentum of the wreck caused the police cruiser to smash into the back of the drunkard's car. Langley could do nothing to prevent his cataclysmic collision with the asphalt. After ten yards he stopped tumbling and came to rest on the roadway, limbs splayed and head spinning.

Breathing...I'm still breathing. Langley blinked and did not dare to move. A horn was blaring ceaselessly, the smell of burnt rubber, oil and blood filled his nostrils.

Langley's vision was twisting wildly; he was on his back staring up at the early morning sky. It had been only seconds, but the accident replayed itself in slow motion through his head as he fought to stay conscious. Time slowed as Langley struggled for each gasp of air.

"*Langley!*" Woods was screaming, sheer panic setting his voice an octave higher than normal. Langley focused on Woods' voice in an attempt to rationalize what was happening around him, but Langley realized he was losing the battle when he couldn't bring himself to take another breath out of fear of the excruciating pain.

He heard boots on the asphalt. Someone was yelling. Then he heard a woman's voice, rough but soothingly melodic. Langley sucked in a small, painful breath as he tried to focus on the new voice, but his eyes felt as if they were fragmenting into his skull, like he was underwater. He groaned, attempting to lift his right arm towards the sky.

"*Langley!*" Woods' voice rose above the road noise; he repeated the cry every few seconds. "*Langley!*"

Someone else was screaming nonsensically and Langley desperately wanted to tell them to shut up. He closed his eyes but opened them when he felt himself falling prey to overwhelming dizziness. He knew he must have a concussion and some broken bones. He did not want to entertain the thought of having to retch in his current condition.

"Langley—you're Langley. It's okay, they've called fire and AMR."

Langley tried to focus on the face now blocking the dusty sky: blue eyes that bore into his, sandy brown hair pulled back from her round face and a soft, small mouth. Lashes so long they nearly touched her curved eyebrows. The face above him became a blur as Langley's vision spiraled.

"You'll be okay, stay with me." Her voice was calming.

As Langley blinked, he felt her hands rest carefully on his shoulder and head. Only then did he realize his entire body was convulsing. Her warm hands helped placate the chill that had been setting in. Langley focused on the places where her skin met his, using her touch as motivation to stay conscious and fight back against the darkness that was taunting his mind.

He inhaled a trace of lavender and he groaned in small pleasure as the horn finally stopped blaring. It was eerily quiet now; Langley listened to the rapid breathing of the woman perched above him and he shifted again, trying to ease the intense stabbing in his left side. He started to choke, realized it was his own blood in his mouth and he turned his head with an involuntary cough. The movement was so excruciating he began to pant, letting the blood dribble down his cheek and into his ear.

"Don't try to move, you'll injure yourself further."

"Nnn....no..."

"Ssshhh! Don't talk."

"Mmmm..."

She pressed a finger to his lips and his stomach tightened involuntarily. He stared up at her and could see her flushed cheeks before his vision blurred again.

"That's better. Look, they're almost here. You'll be alright, Langley." Langley felt something soft wipe his cheek and nose. He regained control for a moment and was able to see his blood smeared on her arm. He could just make out her face above him.

Her cheeks were rosy and Langley noticed a splattering of light freckles around her slender nose. She was poised and calm as she looked off into the distance. Pain grabbed hold of Langley and he tried once more to relieve the pressure on his side but she grabbed his trembling hand with a firm grip and forced it back onto his own stomach. It felt as if a knife were wedged between his mangled ribs.

Her skin was hot against his; he grimaced as she held his hand down, causing the fierce pain in his ribs to worsen. It was torturous to take in the smallest of breaths.

Please, he silently begged. His eyes were hazy, wet. *Just get whatever it is out from under me.*

She finally turned to look at him and for a moment her eyes met his. She leaned closer, her blue eyes suddenly clear in Langley's vision. Langley could do nothing but silently plead for relief from whatever was still crushing his ribs as he felt himself start to shallowly hyperventilate.

She suddenly released his hand. He felt her hand slide delicately across his muscled abdomen. His stomach flexed in response and he grunted inadvertently from the stab of pain he'd caused himself. She calmly slid her hand over his rib cage and Langley moaned, wounded muscles quivering beneath the heat of her fingers.

The woman lightly traced around his mangled ribs until her hand crept underneath him. She slowly slid her hand down from his upper back until she reached his hip. She carefully eased his holster forward, releasing the pressure on his ribs where the grip of his weapon had been jammed between the asphalt and his back. It still hurt like hell, but the momentary relief on that part of his broken body made him want to hug the woman.

"Tthh..."

She put a finger on his lips to silence him as she looked into his eyes once more. "You're welcome."

He heard the wail of the ambulance and he squeezed his eyes shut to try to block out the painful noise. It was too much, and he succumbed to the darkness as the woman's image began to fade.

CHAPTER TWO

It took four days for the hospital to finally release David Langley. Three fractured ribs, a serious concussion, twenty or so stitches, a sprained knee and a separated shoulder was the lasting damage aside from road rash and a collection of horrific bruises; another six weeks at least until he would be mostly healed. In a sling and with a cane, he hobbled out of the white-wall hospital to find Officer Woods, the Chief of Police and a small gang of microphones and recorders waiting for him. He cringed, but there was nothing he could do as the Chief took his good hand and embraced him in a light and awkward hug. At least there were no cameras, for that Langley was thankful.

"Detective Langley!"
"How are you feeling?"
"Do you remember what happened?"
"What are you going to do now?"

Langley took a deep breath and put on his best smile for the Chief, whose anxiety was palpable.

"Ladies and gentlemen, I am thrilled to be alive, safe, and with all my parts still mostly intact. If it weren't for the help of my fellow service members and some beautiful good

Samaritans, I don't think I'd be standing here before you—" *Did I really just say beautiful?* "—so not only do I thank the community for their support and faith in the Police Department, I also thank you all for helping us in our times of need."

The Chief actually sighed aloud.

"That's it folks. That will be all." The Chief announced, waving the reporters away. Officer Woods clasped Langley's hand.

"God Langley, I thought you were dead."

"Close," Langley nodded. "But I'm too stubborn to die."

"Damn Marines. Indestructible bastards."

"Thank you."

"That wasn't a compliment."

"Admit it; if I hadn't shown up, you would have been in the hospital instead of me."

"No doubt in my mind. You seriously saved my ass."

"Langley," The Chief interjected, putting a hand gently on Langley's less-injured shoulder. The Chief's mustache was graying, but the beefy man still commanded attention when he spoke. "You know we've got a ton of paperwork to do, and I understand you need some time to—"

"No problem, Chief. I plan on being at the station tomorrow morning."

"Christ, kid, you've got two weeks off at minimum. You need to heal. There's nothing that can't wait until then."

Langley licked his lips. Going home to an empty refrigerator and a barren apartment didn't sound as good as hanging out with the fellows at the station. Langley's jaw clenched as he nodded.

"Great. Glad you're still among the living, Detective."

"Thanks Chief." With that, the Chief squeezed Langley's solid shoulder and took off back to his own vehicle. Woods was leaning on the door of a new patrol car, looking expectantly at Langley.

"You crash your car and get a new one within a week. Is that policy now?" Langley asked as he hobbled slowly over to the passenger door and opened it.

"Correction: *your* head broke my windshield, so I get a loaner until they repair the damage *your* hulking anatomy did to my car. Do you need help?"

"No. I just need to figure this out—" Langley hit his cane on the computer console on his way in and immediately crumpled into the seat with a yelp. Langley took a few shaky breaths while Woods waited, staring intently at Langley as if he were a ticking time bomb. "I need to work on that," Langley grimaced.

"Your cane just tried to run a license plate. Here," Woods helped Langley right himself and buckled the seat belt over his sling.

"I hate this."

"At least you live in a downstairs apartment."

"Want to help me into the shower, too?"

"About as much as I want to get hit by a patrol car, Detective."

Woods fumbled with his own seat belt a moment before Langley spoke again.

"Where is my truck?"

"I had the pleasure of driving it back to your place." Woods fished in his shirt pocket and produced a set of keys which he pressed into Langley's hand. "Your weapon is with Otter at the armory. Some of your stuff went into evidence; what they didn't want is in the bag in the back."

They drove in silence, listening to the occasional

chatter on the police radio.

Getting out of the car was just as brutal. Langley took his time and let Woods open the front door for him.

"Seriously, are you sure you're okay? Is there anyone I can call for you?"

"I'm good. Really." *Besides, there's no one to call.*

"Well if you need anything..."

Langley cocked his head at the officer, taking the paper bag from Woods' hands. Woods shrugged, sighing.

"I owe you, David. Thank you."

Langley forced a smile as Woods sauntered back to his cruiser.

David Langley shut the door and slowly turned, cane clunking on the entryway tile. He scanned the contents of the bag, then shuffled over to the sagging couch to dump the wallet, badge, empty holster, medical wraps and medications onto the cushions. He grabbed the three pill bottles with his free hand and made his way to the bedroom.

The bed was made, the dresser bare. Just visible on the far side of the bed was a folding chair and the only item that provided a glimpse into Langley's past: a weathered cello, once owned by his late father. This was the cello that had wooed Langley's mother during a concert in Minsk—and resulted in the unexpected creation of one David Langley. Langley had been pushed to follow in his father's footsteps, taking years of lessons and eventually joining his father on the stage for one performance in Vitebsk during the summer of his eighteenth birthday.

Throbbing pain pushed the memories aside; Langley turned, noticing he'd left his closet doors open. His uniforms hung crisp and neat in his closet above two pairs of black boots polished to glassy perfection. Langley's Marine Corps dress blues were in front, ribbons and badges still inspection-ready. Behind was his collection of police uniforms, all pressed and starched. He left the closet open and made his way into the restroom.

The counter was pristine. It was a pet peeve, Langley couldn't help it. His messy x-girlfriend had moved out a year earlier and his apartment had been cleanly preserved ever since. Resting his cane against the counter, he popped open the pill bottles, counted out his allotment and dropped them into his mouth. Using his hand as a cup, he flushed down the mouthful of medications with a swig of tap water.

For the first time since the wreck, he looked at himself in a mirror. His copper eyes drooped heavily, itchy stubble covered his square jaw. There was a barely-healing gash above his ear that sliced through his dark brown, tightly faded hair. He had blue and yellowing bruises on his pallid face and some purple splotches on his arms. With a sigh, Langley carefully removed the sling and placed it on the counter.

Langley delicately pried the button-up shirt away from his torso. It took minutes to get all the buttons undone, but he was thankful someone had been thoughtful enough to supply him that instead of a regular shirt. He cringed just thinking about trying to get clothes off over his head.

His right shoulder was a swirl of purple and reddish-brown. The cuts on his hands and arms were scabbed over, but road rash still covered his forearms and elbows. He flexed his fingers and touched his rib cage where his service pistol had smashed into his ribs as he'd hit the asphalt. Red and purple still pooled there above his hip. His body looked alien to him; he could tell he'd lost at least fifteen pounds and his once-toned physique was more gaunt than he preferred.

Closing his eyes, Langley immediately dismissed the

decrepit image of himself in the mirror. Instead, he envisioned *her,* the woman that had haunted his thoughts and dreams since the wreck and during his entire stay at the hospital. Langley had secretly hoped to see her among his few visitors when he'd regained consciousness, but only his fellow detectives had stopped in.

He pictured her blue eyes, could still feel the tenderness of her touch. She'd known just what to do for Langley at that moment after the wreck; Langley was set on thanking her someday for being the one to help him when he was at his most vulnerable, thank her for inciting his willpower to keep breathing.

Langley opened his eyes and faced his reflection once more. He was exhausted; although the medication took the edge off of the pain, there was still a full-body ache that was overwhelming. He unbuttoned the loose jeans, gingerly pulled off his shoes and slid out of his pants.

In just his boxers, he reattached the sling. Grabbing his cane, he limped to the bed and laid himself on top of the blankets. He pushed a pillow under his knee and closed his eyes, picturing long lashes over blue eyes as he surrendered to a fitful sleep.

CHAPTER THREE

THE NEXT TEN DAYS WERE pure hell. Langley spent most of his time sleeping and tried to keep down the take-out food he ordered daily, though he was often unsuccessful. He knew his body was healing, albeit slowly, and it drove him mad to be cooped up inside and mostly bed-ridden. He'd already lost twenty pounds and his pants fell off without a belt. He numbly went through the physical therapy regiments given to him by the doctor, but nothing seemed to help the constant ache in his ribs.

He mindlessly watched TV when awake and tried to block out the reenactment of the wreck his mind kept trying to dredge up. He'd wake up in a sweat, gasping painfully at imaginary screeching brakes, blinding headlights and the dizzying whirlwind of sky and asphalt.

Langley expected as much: the trauma, the brain's rehashing of such a catastrophic event and the body's involuntary physiological reaction. He'd been through it since the Corps; this was nothing new to him. Knowing didn't make it any easier when the nightmares occurred, but Langley accepted that it was just another notch in his personal belt of fucked-up-ness, another scar on his mind that others couldn't see.

Langley was seeing headlights when the banging at his door snapped him out of his dream. It took three minutes to get up and answer it as his knees were shaking from both the nightmare and his lack of decent nutrition.

"You look like hell." It was Larry Greer, a fellow narcotics detective. "Barnes is out in the car, she wasn't sure it was safe to come up—and by the looks of you, it isn't."

"I think I'm going to puke," Langley groaned, leaning heavily against his door frame. He then realized he was only in his boxers.

Seeing the look of consternation, Greer laughed and grabbed Langley's arm.

"We brought food, but you're going to need to cover up what's left of your six pack so Barnes doesn't get any ideas. She thinks I'm sexier than you and you'll ruin my chances."

Langley inhaled sharply. "Greer, don't make me laugh, everything still hurts."

"Right, sorry."

It took nearly fifteen minutes to get Langley dressed, moderately presentable and seated on the couch. Barnes came to the door with boxes of take-out; the beautiful smell of barbecue filled the air.

"You look fabulous, Marine."

"You guys didn't have to—"

"Shut up, Langley. It's not every month someone gets hit by a car in the department."

Langley eagerly took the box that Barnes offered. Wielding the spoon, he started shoveling food into his mouth.

"So...we watched Woods' dash cam footage," Greer said, taking a bite from his plate. "That was some serious shit. And that Navy chick, she really took it to—"

"Navy chick?" Langley paused his shoveling, staring at Greer.

"Yeah, the woman that helped Woods get the handcuffs on the drunken bastard after you got hit."

"Wait, who?"

"The first person on the scene, the one that was with you."

"Really?"

"Where have you been? She only stayed with you for five minutes until you were loaded into the ambulance, and she even followed you to the damn hospital."

"Seriously?"

"God, you don't remember?" Barnes whispered.

"I remember—" *deep blue eyes, lavender and the warmth of her touch...* "I mean, I remember seeing her for a second, yeah." Langley glared. "I had just gotten hit by a car, so excuse me if my memory is a little fuzzy. I was unconscious for most of that." Langley commenced his shoveling once again and they sat in silence until Langley finished his plate.

"We bought you a week's worth of this stuff. Well, in your case probably two days worth, but at least you've got some food in this place now."

"Thanks, Mom."

Barnes stuck her tongue out like a ten year old would, and she put the remainder of the food in his fridge.

"Lieutenant Miller says take your time, you don't need to come in for at least another week," Greer leaned against the wall as he tugged at his goatee.

"I'd like to see the dash cam video. And I have a ton of paperwork and reports to do. And I need to get the hell out of this apartment."

"Suit yourself."

They helped Langley gather his effects and cane. Greer walked in front of Langley protectively, scanning the apartment complex as Langley locked his door.

Barnes chatted amiably on the ride, gingerly touching Langley's thigh from time to time. She was cute: red curly hair, a fiery personality and a tight, perky body that was complimented by a radiant smile. She was rough around the edges and a little too aggressive for Langley. She'd hit him up for a date a year ago; Langley had politely declined. In fact, he'd been asked out by all of the girls in Admin, the K-9 units and even the Police Chief's hot personal secretary, much to the chagrin of all the single men working the station. But he'd courteously denied them all, touting his focus on his career as the excuse.

In reality, he was avoiding all women associated with the force. He'd tried long ago, and it had never worked out for long. The combination of departmental politics, mistrust, overbearing protectiveness and too much alpha personality within the relationship never resulted in anything pleasant. Reminiscing made Langley shudder as Barnes kept talking during the ride, oblivious to Langley's detachment.

But his luck hadn't improved when dating outside the force, either. Women kept trying to treat him like a trophy or a trump card simply because he had a badge and a gun, or they were intimidated by the unpredictability and general horrors of his job.

Langley shook his head and smirked. Being single certainly had advantages. Beer stayed in the fridge, the bathroom was always squared away. He never had to worry about someone using his razor, either. Life was calmer and he was accountable to no one; and yet, a fleeting image of the woman's beautiful face above him at the wreck made him ponder whether he actually *did* want to remain single.

I don't, his mind instantly decided.

Langley was greeted by a lot of hearty handshakes and applause when he entered the station. It took ten minutes to make his way to the armory where a woman nearly as tall as him was waiting behind the cage, scrutinizing his cane.

"Well well, if it ain't the human pinball!"

"Nice to see you too, Otter. Now give me my gun." Otter rolled her eyes as she turned to get his pistol. She was nearly as wide as Langley too, and she prided herself on being able to leg press somewhere near 800 pounds. He did not want to ever be on her bad side.

"Here you go." She handed him his weapon and his magazine. She tilted her head, eyebrow raised as she examined him. Although he'd ditched the sling, Langley still cradled his arm protectively. "You want a drop holster for the time being? You look pretty banged up. I have one lefty, just for you."

"Yes, thanks."

It took some help to get him adjusted, but he felt better having his pistol back at his side. His gun hand was still functioning and he did not like being unarmed.

On his desk was a pile of papers and post-it notes. He scanned over the paperwork, but was spared having to sort through it when Lieutenant Miller came around the corner.

"David! Welcome back." They shook hands. Miller took a step back to look Langley up and down. "You've gained some weight, I see."

"Very funny, Lieutenant."

"I've got the reports started for you from the wreck. I need you to do that first and foremost so we can close that up. Have you seen the footage yet?"

"No, sir."

"Meet me in my office."

"Will do."

Langley fingered through the files on his desk. Most were from the drug case they'd been working for months, dealing with a big ring of drug-dealing biker-gang members. He pushed that all to the side, hoping to find something interesting. He began to look at the notes. One post-it read "Red Bull gives you wiiiiiings!" Another, "You should have joined the Air Force."

Langley shook his head and looked up. He could hear snickering coming from a few of his fellow officers around the unit.

"Ha, ha. Hilarious." He gathered the post-its into a neat group and set them in his desk drawer.

Seeing nothing pertinent, Langley made his way to the Lieutenant's office. He was getting better with the stupid cane, but he couldn't wait until he could throw it in the dumpster.

"Have a seat, Detective."

Langley lowered himself into the uncomfortable folding chair.

The Lieutenant had to go through a litany of questions and paper work, making sure that Langley was in a stable state of mind and would pass a psyche evaluation. It took fifteen minutes until the Lieutenant finally tossed his pen and picked up the TV remote.

"Now, the pièce de résistance!" Miller turned on the TV and switched the settings, bringing to view a brightly lit scene via dash cam.

Langley watched as Officer Woods began the traffic stop. He listened to the radio traffic, watched the big drunk get out of his car as Langley pinged in on the radio. The drunk man took a swing at Woods; when it didn't connect, the drunk grabbed onto Woods and tried pulling whatever he could grab out of Woods' belt. They struggled for nearly thirty seconds before Langley heard the tires of his own vehicle. He heard himself yell, then saw his body charge into view, taking the DUI suspect by the arm.

After Langley shoved the man onto the dirt shoulder, Woods darted off camera. There was a peaceful pause as Langley just stood there, looking towards Woods.

Langley realized he was holding his breath and forced his lungs to expel air.

His mind was not prepared to hear the squealing tires once again and a whimper involuntarily escaped his lips. He watched his head turn on the video, saw the whites of his own eyes, and then the patrol car lurched forward; he watched his body smash into the windshield and block the camera, then saw through the shattered glass as the cars collided. His body flew forward as the suspect's car spun into traffic. The patrol car had turned a bit to show both the road and the shoulder now. Langley could see himself lying on the asphalt on the left side of the frame and he saw Woods still wielding the taser through a piece of unbroken windshield. The non-stop horn of the crashed SUV drowned out all other audio.

Then the drunk dragged himself into view and Woods tased him again. Then he saw her—a woman wearing a gray long-sleeve sweater and jeans came sprinting into view. She was fairly petite and slender, but she rivaled Woods in athleticism. As the next five second taser ride ended, Woods and the woman pounced onto the man together, getting him swiftly cuffed. The drunk lay wriggling in the dirt. Langley watched Woods pointing towards his body lying in the roadway, and the woman immediately ran over to him. *Unafraid of drunk men twice her size? The woman is fearless.*

He realized he was holding his breath again and let out a rush of air.

She had ran to him, immediately dropped to her knees and from what Langley could tell she was checking his pulse. She put her face near his and was speaking. Finally the horn cut off, and he could hear Woods yelling into his radio while periodically screaming Langley's name. The driver of the SUV was still screaming something unintelligible; Woods sat him down on the shoulder and politely told him to shut his mouth.

"I look pretty dead."

"You'd make a very attractive corpse, Detective."

They stopped talking as the sirens came into hearing range of the dash cam. Langley squinted to try and see the woman better, but to no avail. He could hear sirens, non-stop radio traffic and Woods. Langley sighed, wishing he could have a better glimpse of her, or to hear her voice again. He watched her reach under him and shift his weapon forward, then Langley remembered this was the point where he had passed out.

Greer was right. The woman did stay with him; she had even been holding his hand and cradling his head in her arm before they finally lifted him into the ambulance a minute later.

Damn. I couldn't be conscious for that?

He watched the ambulance take off and then watched her jog casually over to Woods. She scribbled something on a piece of paper Woods had given her and shoved it back into Woods' hands. Langley watched her run towards and then past the dash cam.

The next four minutes was radio traffic and Woods loading drunk #1 and possible SUV drunk driver #2 into the back of other patrol cars. The footage went black.

Miller sat back in his chair.

"You know you've been put in for the Police Purple Heart."

Langley blinked, still digesting the words. "That's ridiculous. It's not like I threw myself into the path of the car on purpose. Nor did I save anyone in the process."

"It's been a while since this department has had such a tragic incident involving one of our own. Officer Woods is up for the Medal of Valor, and your little guardian angel there is up for the meritorious civilian service award, though she already turned it down."

"Turned it down?"

"Said she wasn't interested. Didn't even give us her full name on the report, though she did give us a nicely detailed statement."

"Who is she?"

Miller's brow arched and he smiled widely. "A former Navy Corpsman. That's right, Marine—because us Navy personnel are always there to pick up the pieces after you Marines destroy everything."

CHAPTER FOUR

IT TOOK TWO HOURS BEFORE Langley was done typing out the six page report. It was obnoxiously time consuming for him to read (and reread) his report until he was satisfied that he had not forgotten anything.

He couldn't stop thinking about the video; not the crash, but the parts that Langley *didn't* remember on account of being unconscious. To have a complete stranger escort him into an ambulance and then follow him to the hospital; well, that seemed far above and beyond what any average civilian would have done.

Langley did a recorded interview with some internal affairs suits, signed a lot of medical paperwork, and then went over evidence pictures, procedures and protocols. The sun was starting to go down when Officer Woods strolled over to Langley's desk in the Narcotics Unit.

"Detective Langley! Heard you were in and I wanted to offer you a ride home."

"I'm about ready," Langley was sitting at his computer, flipping through the new reports without much concentration. He stacked the papers as neatly as possibly, then rose with his cane firmly in one hand.

As they strolled out of the station, Langley tapped Woods on the leg with his cane. Woods paused outside the door and looked quizzically at Langley.

"That paper, the sheet of paper you gave the woman..." Langley stammered. He cleared his throat and took a deep, painful breath. "What did you have the woman at the wreck write on the paper?"

"I asked her for her number," Woods said innocently. Langley's hand gripped the cane tightly, knuckles white. "No, seriously, I wanted to be able to call her if the Captain needed anything other than her statement."

"Go on."

"She told me she wanted as little publicity as possible, so that was all she offered. You know, she was fearless when she helped me cuff the drunk, but when I started taking down her statement she got," Woods scratched his cheek pensively, "well, weird. Clammed up." Woods stopped talking, his eyes flicking down to Langley's hands. "Why?"

"I'd like to thank her. It seems only fair."

Woods glanced around, finally emitting a sigh. "If anyone asks me, you stole it out of my notebook."

"Understood."

Woods dug into his shirt pocket and extracted his notepad. He opened it and slid a finger into the small front pocket. He withdrew a crumpled piece of paper among many, handed it to Langley and immediately turned to walk towards his patrol car.

Langley leaned on the cane to follow slowly behind Woods. He was much more careful getting into the car this time, and they made it to Langley's apartment without incident.

David thanked Woods and fumbled for his keys. He dropped his cane inside the door and limped to the couch where he flopped down. He pulled out the crumpled paper and slowly unfolded it, breathing heavily.

It was just a name: Jenna. And then seven scribbled digits below it.

"Jenna." Langley said out loud, letting the name roll off his tongue. He grabbed his cell phone and dialed the first five numbers, then froze.

And if she reports me for harassment?

He argued with himself, going back and forth. It was eight o'clock at night. Maybe he'd be interrupting something, maybe she was asleep, maybe it was a fake number?

Wuss.

Langley pressed the last two numbers and hit send.

Ring.

Ring.

Ring.

"Patty's Diner, how can I help you?"

Langley hesitated and then quickly responded. "Wrong number."

"Good night then!"

"'Night." Langley hung up, a growl emerging from his throat. He checked the number; he'd dialed correctly. The woman Jenna had given Woods the number to a cheap local eatery.

Langley threw the phone onto the couch and hobbled to the bedroom. He stripped and took a long, hot shower. The soreness had mostly faded away; now it was his knee and ribs that continued to bother him. Annoyed, he made his way to his bed and sank into the mattress.

6:37

Langley had watched the clock for twenty minutes

before accepting that there would be no more sleep for him. He took his time getting ready; it was still only 7:15 by the time he was prepared for the drive to work, but he didn't have to be there for another three and a half hours.

He was hungry. Pausing only for a moment, he decided to go and eat a big, greasy breakfast in celebration of being alive.

That, and Patty's Diner still was a point of interest for him. The curiosity was nagging at him more than the pit in his stomach.

Driving was still tricky given that his knees were still tender, especially the sprained right. But the swelling had finally gone down and he could strap the supporting knee brace around it, which almost eliminated the need for the cane. A few more days and he'd be able to limp around without it.

Patty's Diner was open at five in the morning, allowing truckers and the early morning crowd a place to read the paper and drink coffee. Langley—dressed in loose fitting jeans, a dark gray and subtly flannel button-up, a pair of comfortable boots with a pair of dark sunglasses perched on his nose—entered the diner and had a seat in a back corner of the bar area so he could have a full view of the place. And a clear path to the exit, which was most important.

He rested his cane against his thigh, flipped the sunglasses around to rest on the back of his skull. Some of the patrons stared a little too long, their eyes lingering on the ghastly scar above his ear. Langley coolly ignored them all. An elderly woman came to take his order as he glanced at the first page of the menu.

"What'll it be, darlin'?"

"Country omelet, no cheese and decaf, please."

"You got it." The woman retreated before she even

finished writing. Langley pretended to scan the disheveled newspaper before him; instead, he observed the patrons.

No threats, and he certainly wasn't eager for any. He was covertly hoping a sandy brown ponytail would come into view at any moment.

It occurred to him sometime during the previous night that not everyone had a cell phone, and this Jenna may want no ties to her home. Therefore, Langley deduced that the phone number she'd given Woods was likely to be a work number. The detective knew that it would be much more acceptable if he just happened to come in contact with her in a public setting as opposed to hounding her on the only number she'd provided to the police department.

A cup of coffee was slid in front of Langley. He sipped it black, enjoying the bitterness, scanning the room constantly. Two servers came out from the kitchen, one a lanky man with black shaggy hair and the other—

Langley's breath caught in his chest, causing a twinge of pain in his ribs which made him grit his teeth. She hadn't looked his way yet. Langley hastily lifted the newspaper, staring over the page to watch her as she strolled past the bar where he sat.

The serving apron did her tight body no justice. Langley had seen many attractive women in his thirty years of life, but there was something about the way her hips moved that put all the others to shame. Her back was taunt as she walked, like a cat ready to pounce. She exuded confidence, enough to make Langley wonder if he was making the right decision confronting her.

Jesus, I'm a coward.

Langley scowled, annoyed with his own apprehension. Langley steeled himself and waited for her to come back around the diner.

CHAPTER FIVE

JENNA WAS EXHAUSTED. It had been a long two weeks of mind-numbing, unrewarding work. Not to mention her brother Frank had been overwhelmingly micro-managing in the past few weeks because of her recent contact with law enforcement.

Ever since their father's police abuse case ten years prior, when she and Frank were just teens, it was a never-ending stream of fury from him. Her brother *hated* cops, and he thought everyone else should hate them just as much as he did.

Granted, Jenna had similar sentiments; after seeing her father almost beaten to death before her eyes, she had no love for anyone on the force and certainly didn't want to come in contact with cops on any level. But the wreck had been different; Jenna had tried to explain to her brother that she was utilizing her training as a corpsman to render support and help stabilize the man, but he heard nothing other than that she'd willingly put herself into the middle of a police situation she had no reason or obligation to be in.

It was no use fighting; her brother believed all cops were bad and that this man was no different. But for God's sake, the man had just been hit by a *car,* and the other officer was in serious distress. And how could she live with herself if she just drove past the scene because it *wasn't her problem?* Her brother would never understand.

Jenna was in the diner filling up an angry customer's morning coffee as she thought back to the wreck.

She wasn't supposed to have worked that morning, but a fellow employee had called her late the night before and begged her to open the diner, so Jenna had been on the road by four fifteen that morning. She was driving a ways behind the SUV that had swerved into the patrol car, and then witnessed the resulting crash. Jenna had parked behind a truck with her hazard lights on when she'd seen the uniformed officer struggling to subdue a larger man. Once Jenna helped him cuff the drunk driver, the officer started frantically screaming out a name; only then did she notice the plain-clothes cop lying in the roadway.

That had been a rough morning; her brother had refused to stop calling her cell while she had been trying to make sure the man—Langley, it was—made it to the hospital. Once she ensured he was stabilized with the nurse's affirmation that he'd likely live, she went to leave but was stopped by the other officer from the wreck; she had quickly given him a statement and then ran out of the hospital as more police cars packed into the ER parking lot, all of them rushing to check on their wounded colleague.

Then she'd almost gotten fired for showing up to work late, three hours after she was supposed to clock in and open the restaurant. And her phone had kept ringing all day, so she had thrown the damn cell phone in the trash on the way home, thankful she'd given the cops the number to the diner. The last thing Jenna wanted was media attention, especially in light of her brother's severe anxiety. She also didn't want to dredge up the memories of her father's case.

Coffee full, she strolled out of the kitchen with a fellow server, putting on a face of determination that didn't reflect her inner strife.

As she walked, she let her mind wander. The man had been *conscious*. And although he'd been badly banged up, Jenna could vividly remember the fiery look in his bronze eyes.

She'd seen plenty of wounded Marines during her time in the Navy; the cop was no different in that regard. Seeing that cop injured in the road made for an eerie déjàvus, bringing back all Jenna's tense memories of young men trembling beneath her hands as she consoled and tried to heal them.

None of those men had been quite like Langley, however. She'd seen nothing but fierce resolve in his eyes that day; no fear, even as he lay bleeding in her arms. His determination and grit, his intense will to survive, was something that Jenna had only seen a few times in her life. It was something most people could only allude to without having witnessed it themselves.

She remembered the coppery twinge to his eyes, the way his body shook uncontrollably under her touch. Jenna had never felt so vulnerable herself, still deciphering her haunting memories of his eyes boring into hers, making her breath catch. At his worst, lying broken on the asphalt, the man had managed to addle Jenna's emotions in a way that no one, no man, had ever done before.

The other officer had been beside himself, screaming Langley's name repeatedly until the ambulance arrived. He'd been shaking almost as hard as Langley. Jenna had witnessed the deep brotherly bond between them, the desperation of not being able to do anything when a person you care deeply for is battling for life. *Frank could never understand.*

This man Langley surely had no idea who she was. *Why does it matter, and why do I care so much?* Jenna sighed, chiding herself.

"Here you go," Jenna delivered the coffee and made a quick round, coming back to the bar to see if any of her orders were up.

None were. She drummed her fingers lightly on the counter, chewing her lip as she waited, soaking up the moment of silence.

"Jenna?"

God, I'm not your server and I don't want to get you coffee! Jenna sighed before turning.

"Yes?"

Only then did she realize who had called her name. He wore long sleeves, but she could see the bulk of his muscular physique under the flannel shirt. His hair was cut short and his eyes were the color of whiskey with radiating golden-brown streaks. He sported a few days worth of auburn stubble over his strong jaw line and he definitely looked thinner than the last time she'd seen him. Jenna saw the faint yellow of the fading bruises and the healing gash above his ear.

He looked at her fiercely, like a hawk closing in on his prey.

"Oh my God."

"Is it that bad?"

Jenna was mortified. "No! No, I didn't mean—"

"I'm sorry," he interjected. "I just wanted to quickly thank you, you know, for what you did for me." Jenna stared at him a moment, watched him shift slowly in his seat.

"I...oh, well, you're welcome, Mr. Langley." Jenna

couldn't figure out what to do with her hands as they seemed to flit about on their own.

"David."

"What?"

"My name is David."

"David." Jenna clasped her hands together in front of her, trying to stop the trembling. *What's the matter with me?* "It's good to see you." *Oh Lord, did I really just...* "I mean, good to see you up. You know, healing."

"I'm on the mend." He smiled, a radiant flashing of white teeth. "I'm sorry if I interrupted you at work," He slid his hand forward on the bar, relaxed. "I don't want to keep you, but if there is anything I can ever do to return the favor..."

Oh, my. Jenna's eyebrows arched as she licked the inside of her lip. "That's not necessary, just you telling me that is enough. And thank you. You know, for thanking me." *God I'm an idiot!*

He nodded once as he smirked, making Jenna's breath catch. He idly tapped his fingertips on the bar.

"Then I suppose it's my turn to say you're welcome."

All Jenna could do was force a smile—to prevent herself from saying anything more ridiculous than she already had. Jenna felt her cheeks get hot as he stared at her. He brought both his hands together and touched his lips with his index fingers. The gesture sent her heart fluttering. *He's a cop!* Her mind was screaming. But her heart was betraying her on account of his dazzling smile and warm, comforting eyes.

Jenna was angry at herself for losing control of her emotions, irritated by her blubbering responses. No man had ever turned her into a blithering idiot, and she couldn't believe that the one to do it would be a *cop*, the type of people she despised most on account of their dominating personalities and over-inflated egos; she braced herself, allowing her annoyance with her own foolishness to take control.

"Was that all?"

The cop's eyebrows dipped, creasing at the bridge of his nose. He sat back in his chair, shrugging one shoulder while dropping his hands back to the bar.

"I suppose it is," His head tilted slightly. "Thank you, Jenna."

The way he said her name made her stomach flutter. His voice was deep—gruff and calm at the same time, a man in control. Jenna cleared her throat, trying to regain her own composure. The bell dinged behind her, and she turned to find a meal placed on the chef's counter. *An escape!*

She grabbed the tag and the plate, ready to dash off to take a moment to compose herself. She looked at the table number...and wanted to slap herself.

It was his.

"Enjoy your breakfast," she nearly threw the plate on the bar.

He regarded her evenly, his gaze never wandering from her face. She felt like an animal in a zoo; she turned to leave and knew that he was still watching her as she practically ran to the kitchen.

Jenna stopped as she rounded the corner, smacking the back of her head as she leaned heavily against the wall. *I'm such an ass.* Breathing heavily, she growled aloud. The cop had only tried to thank her and she had turned into a stammering fool, then a defensive jerk.

Of course she had fantasized about seeing him again, but not at the diner and certainly not while she was covered in old grease and coffee. And she had certainly *not* expected the fantasy to become a reality.

She stared at the back exit. Rubbing her arms with her hands, she took a moment to make the decision to at least repair some of the damage she'd done. *It's not like he was trying to ask me out, he was just trying to thank me.*

Straightening herself, she brushed the wisps of hair from her face. With poise, she walked back to the front of the diner and over to the bar...

...only to see an untouched plate and thirty dollars sitting underneath an empty coffee cup.

Frantic, she cased the diner looking for David Langley, but he wasn't there. She hurried to the front door. Jenna saw him leaning on his cane, unlocking the door to a truck. She wanted to run to him and apologize, to tell him how thoughtful it was that he'd come to thank her. Tell him how much she'd secretly been waiting for that exact moment when she would see him again. And tell him how much she wanted to hold his hand again and tell him everything would be alright.

Instead, she stood there, staring out the grease-smudged door as her eyes misted over.

"Hey Janet—Jane, whatever! I need more coffee!"

Jenna emitted a quiet whimper as she watched him start his truck and drive out of the parking lot. She went to the back and grabbed a pot of coffee, resigned to the fact that she was about to have a very shitty day.

CHAPTER SIX

LANGLEY DROVE TO A DRIVE thru and ordered a hamburger at eight in the morning. *That did not go well*, he thought to himself. He turned the truck's radio to a different station, listening to the symphony of classical instruments as he ordered.

Jenna had seemed terrified to see him. Or maybe terrified *of* him. Either way, the woman had been intensely nervous. *You're a cop,* Langley grimaced to himself. *Nobody likes cops.* Not to mention she seemed completely distracted and uninterested. *You went there to thank her, not to ask her out on a date,* Langley told himself. But he found himself thinking about how she'd look without that apron on. He took a deep breath even though he knew it would make his ribs hurt like hell.

"I said my piece," Langley said to his hamburger, "and now I move on." He devoured the burger and showed up to work an hour early, having nothing better to do. Seeing a new pile of demeaning post-its on his desk, he decided to work on a bit of payback before most of his team came in to work. He was calmly seated in the conference room by the time everyone came in for the morning meeting.

There was a group of fifteen officers, detectives and higher ups, including Langley. He sat in the back, thumping his cane lightly on the carpet, listening to the new announcements and updates that had developed.

"And now, I need Detective Langley front and center."

Langley stopped bouncing his cane and stared at the detective.

"Yes, you, Dr. House. Come on up." Knowing he had no choice, Langley limped to the front of the conference room.

"As a six-year veteran of the Police Department, we'd like to honor your service today by presenting you with a few awards."

"Sounds very legitimate, Detective."

"Firstly, on behalf of everyone here, we would like you to have this."

The man grinned wolfishly as he handed over a poorly wrapped box.

"I just can't wait." Langley shoved the wrapping paper into the chest of the detective as he produced a shoe box. Inside was a well-used pair of Air Jordan's.

"We present to you the Jordan's of Justice—to help you jump higher and achieve greater heights, especially when jumping over cars." There was laughter as Langley pulled the shoes out and set them on the table. "And we also present you the wings of the airman that you should have been, because we all know that Marines can't fly, no matter how hard they try." The detective tried to pin the enormous badge onto Langley's shirt.

"Ah *hell* no! Get that Air Force crap away from me." Langley wielded his cane like a baton, daring the detective to continue his pursuit. The detective laughed heartily, then set the badge down next to the shoes.

"Pipe down Detective, we still have one more award to go. Lastly, we present this—" a bag was picked up from underneath the table, "—so that you may never forget what happened. Not that you could forget it, but we want to remind you every day."

Langley reached into the bag and grabbed a picture frame. Holding it so he could see it first, he shook his head.

It was an old image of him in his police uniform with large, photo-shopped angel wings. There was a caption above the picture that read "Airborne all the way!" It was an utterly time consuming and worthless project, but damn weren't his coworkers proud of it.

Langley flipped it around to show the rest of the team. They all applauded as Langley took a half bow, which was all his ribs would accommodate.

"And now my turn," Langley said, propping the frame on the table. "I'd like to thank you all for wasting so much time honoring my return. Hopefully one of you gets jumped by an overweight transient that hasn't showered in twenty years."

"I give it a week." Greer smiled. "Welcome back, Langley."

Langley went and sat at his desk. He started rifling through the files there, reading up on the intelligence and surveillance his team had gathered in his absence. As he studied, he watched as other detectives sat down at their own desks. Langley waited patiently, taking a steadying breath to keep himself from laughing.

"Hey man, what the hell?" Barnes yelled, banging her computer's mouse down on her desk. She tried to squiggle it violently. "What is *wrong* with this stupid thing?"

Langley covered his laugh with the file folder. She

finally flipped the mouse over, ending her tirade. She pulled a post-it off the bottom of the mouse.

"Langley, you son of a bitch. Like my blood pressure isn't already high enough," Barnes shook her head. Greer slyly checked under his mouse, but there was nothing there. Looking smug, Greer went to shut the open drawer at his desk.

SQUEEAK!

"What the fuck?" Greer recoiled. "If that's a mouse I'm going to finish what the patrol car started on you, Langley." Greer went to shut the drawer again—SQUEEAK!

Greer pulled the drawer so hard that office supplies flew in every direction. He reached back into the empty cavity, fished around a moment and then stood, dog toy raised triumphantly.

Langley lifted his hands, feigning innocence. It was another ten minutes before the inner-station phone rang at Lieutenant Miller's desk. Langley casually got up and limped his way over as if he were headed to the coffee.

Miller picked up the phone.

"Lieutenant Miller."

BRRRING!

"Shit."

BRRRING!

He slammed the phone back down and picked it up again.

BRRRING!

"Jesus what the hell!" Only then did he finally (BRRRING!) notice the tape stuck on the hook of the receiver. He frantically picked it off, answering the phone on its sixth ring.

"Lieutenant Miller." Seeing Langley sipping coffee outside the office, Miller vigorously flipped him off as he continued his call.

Work complete, Langley went back to his desk to enjoy the rest of his day.

Getting back into the groove at work was easy for Langley. Besides, most of his unit's work currently consisted of sitting in cars people-watching and talking with a few informants. The case against the biker gang was getting stronger; the gang had supposedly started dealing some harder drugs—mostly meth and heroin—alongside their usual pot sales at the local biker bar and a few uninvolved patrons had just started reporting the strange activities.

The goal, however, was to nab both the supplier and all the dealers involved. Otherwise, the most important pieces of the puzzle would slip away while simultaneously letting the perpetrators know the cops were tracking their movements. Therefore, the team kept constant surveillance on the bar and some of the senior members of the gang to try and discover the suppliers.

Langley was sitting in an unmarked car with Greer, keeping watch on one of the supposed dealers. It was a slow day, and there was absolutely nothing happening. As Greer manned the radio, Langley's mind drifted. He envisioned a splash of freckles, focused blue eyes and a firm, toned body. Even though she'd completely shunned him at the diner, he still couldn't help but notice how her hands had trembled and how her cheeks had turned red when he thanked her. *God, her hands were so—*

"I think I'm going to the range tonight," Greer drummed his fingers on the steering wheel, snapping Langley out of his trance. "Want to go?"

"Yes, absolutely." Langley answered quickly. He stretched his shoulders up, then back. Langley tightened the strap on his knee brace. He had also vowed today would be the last day for the cane. Most of the surface bruises and scrapes were gone, the stitches had been pulled out. Just the irritating knee pain, tender ribs and a stiff shoulder remained.

He was tired of not being able to do much of anything but sit and stand. Therefore, he would go shooting—even if his shoulder wasn't going to like it.

Langley finished his notes and typed up the day's report in the car. He even finished up Greer's during the drive so they could head immediately to the outdoor range before it shut down for the night.

They packed up an AR-15 and a Remington 870 and got the month's allotment of practice ammo. Fortunately, the range wasn't crowded; Greer and Langley ended up in a bay with only two other officers.

"Mmmmm." Langley closed his eyes, allowing the invigorating smell of CLP, brass and gunpowder to seep into his nostrils. Man, how he missed that smell. He breathed deeply, feeling suddenly revitalized.

They took turns from twenty five yards with their pistols, enjoying the friendly competition even though Langley beat them every round. Rifle was never much fun when shooting a stationary target from a max of thirty yards away, so Langley opted to sit that one out. However, when shotgun came up, Langley hopped up from his seat, cane in hand.

"You know, you really shouldn't use your cane while operating a shotgun," the officer folded his arms over his broad chest, looking over at Langley with pursed lips.

"Thanks for the advice," *Jackass*, Langley added to himself. He held the cane over his shoulder as he limped well past the firing line. Reaching the targets, he set his cane in front of one and hobbled back.

"Now, just what in the hell—"

"Please, just shut up and put your ear pro on." Langley growled, grabbing the shotgun from Greer. He slammed four rounds into the bottom in under two seconds as the officers scrabbled for their ear muffs.

Without preamble, Langley fired all four rounds in quick succession, fragmenting the cane into a number of gnarled pieces. His shoulder hurt like hell, but he didn't care.

"You are one psychotic asshole, Detective." The officer glared at Langley. Greer was laughing in fits, pointing at the officer's scowl. Langley passed the unloaded shotgun to Greer, chuckling.

"Feel better now?" Greer snickered.

"Abso-fucking-lutely."

"Let's get the hell out of here before those suck-ups complain."

Langley helped carry the gear back to the car, limping but happy to be rid of the cane.

The two detectives laughed the whole way back to the station. Langley's ribs were aching from all the activity. After turning the weapons back over to Otter, they started the stroll back to the front door to go home for the night.

"Hey, Langley!"

"Ah, shit." Greer groaned, turning to Langley. "They got you."

"I don't give a—"

"Langley!" Miller was glowering. "Did you really just fire your shotgun at an unapproved metal object on the range?"

"Yes. Yes I did."

Miller looked a little surprised about the open

admission, but recovered instantly.

"Can you explain yourself? At all?"

"Well sir," Langley said, clapping his hands together, "you see, the cane *really* had it coming."

CHAPTER SEVEN

JENNA WAS AT HER BROTHER'S house, filling out more job applications. If she could land another part time job somewhere, she could afford to move out of her brother's ramshackle rental once and for all.

Every paramedic job in the city was filled, so she had to look outside her chosen profession for something. For anything, really. Waitressing was not her cup of tea, but she was doing what she had to do to make ends meet. Although it wasn't enough to change her circumstances, she was determined to do something quickly in an effort to regain her independence.

It had been almost a week since the cop had come into the diner, but she was still thinking about it. In fact, she couldn't *stop* thinking about it.

Jenna's brother had finally calmed down about the whole situation. Now he was back to his usual self: loud, drunk, and obnoxious. She hadn't told him about David Langley coming into her work, and he didn't seem to know about it. And she would make sure it stayed that way. He had said nothing in the past week about the cops at all.

"Hey sis!" His voice boomed from the other side of the

house.

"Yeah?"

"Wanna go to the Saloon with us? We're leaving right now."

"No, thank you. I have to work early."

Jenna heard the front door slam shut. She smiled to herself, letting out a little sigh of relief.

She'd been gathering her courage silently. Jenna knew her brother wouldn't be home for hours; he liked hanging out at the bar until closing, giving Jenna another five or six hours of solitude. Using her brother's house phone, she decided that it was time to give David Langley an apology. Cop or not, the man was only attempting to show his gratitude and she had automatically rejected him for no legitimate reason, other than her own emotional hang-ups.

It was late evening, so she knew he'd be gone for the night. The goal was to leave a brief message, just to tell him that she was sorry for being a total jerk to him at the diner. That was it. Boom, done. Short and to the point, just like she'd done in her head a thousand times. Then that would be the end of David Langley nagging at her every thought.

She dialed the phone number to the police department.

"Brookside Police Department, how may I direct your call?"

"David Langley, please."

"Hold please."

She waited to be connected. The phone began to ring, and she prepared her practiced speech for the answering machine.

Lieutenant Miller stared at Langley as if he were an alien.

"What is *wrong* with you." It seemed like a rhetorical

question so Langley just stood there, looking at his Lieutenant expectantly, taking his ass-chewing in proper, respectful stride. Greer looked towards the door and Langley eyed him sideways; Greer got the message and stayed put.

"I assume you won't do something that dumb again, right?"

"Of course not, sir."

"And that I didn't make a mistake in signing a paper saying that you're emotionally stable, psychologically sane enough to maintain your current position?"

"No mistake, sir."

"Then stop being an idiot. It's my ass too, Langley."

"Sorry sir."

"And if you fuck with my phone again I'll plant a CS canister in your desk."

Langley's response was cut short as one of the desk phones started ringing.

All three of them looked at one another in turn. No one wanted to answer a call this late, especially if it was directed to their unit. It usually meant useless tips and a lot of paperwork.

The Lieutenant abruptly smiled, bouncing on his toes.

"You should get that, Detective. It's probably my boss wanting a piece of you before he goes home for the night."

Langley groaned, but responded with a "Yessir."

He made his way to the phone as quickly as he could manage and picked up the receiver right before the answering machine was set to kick in.

"Detective Langley."

"Ah...David?"

Langley blinked, eyes wide.

"Who is this?" *You know who it is, you dip-shit!*

"It's...it's Jenna."

"I—um—yes?"

"I thought you'd be gone by now."

Langley couldn't understand what she meant by that. "No, I'm still here." Miller and Greer were watching him curiously.

"Oh. Well, I just wanted to tell you I'm sorry. You know, the other morning you came in and I was busy, but I wanted to let you know that I did appreciate...what you said."

Miller took a step towards the desk. Langley held up his hand to stop him, shaking his head.

"Right. Thank you."

"And if you ever do come back in, I owe you breakfast. You didn't even touch yours." Now she spoke with a bit more fluidity, as if she were reading from a script.

"I will keep that in mind."

"Okay then."

"Good night."

"Good night, David."

He set the phone back on the receiver, expression blank. His heart was beating wildly against his tender ribs.

"Who the hell was that?" Miller's voice brought Langley crashing back to reality.

Langley cleared his throat. "Crazy tipster looking for a reward."

Miller frowned. Shrugging, the Lieutenant about-faced and strolled towards the front door.

"Good night, Detectives."

"Night sir," Greer and Langley responded in unison.

Langley limped over to Greer. Together they exited the building, embracing the chill night air. Greer snorted before patting Langley gently on the back.

"It's always a fiasco with you," he chuckled as they sauntered to their vehicles. "Have a good night, Lang."

"Night," Langley unlocked the door of his truck and slid behind the steering wheel. He couldn't even remember the details of the drive home—he was dreaming of blue eyes and a sun-kissed ponytail.

CHAPTER EIGHT

JENNA HUNG UP THE PHONE with finality. She felt light-headed and a little dizzy as she went back to the tiny bedroom in her brother's house that she currently called home. A mattress lay on the ground, a few military bags held most of her clothes and belongings, and a small TV was perched on a dresser. Nothing hung on the walls except one picture of her with her unit in Afghanistan. The picture had been taken one month before her career had abruptly ended and she'd been sent back stateside indefinitely.

It took a four month hospital stay to recover from the damage the ridiculous Humvee crash had caused. Jenna closed her eyes and dwelt on the memory for a minute, replaying it in her mind to push thoughts of David Langley out of her head.

She opened her eyes, scanning the picture one more time before turning back to the mattress, which housed a number of job applications. Jenna sat on the floor and picked up a pen. *Back to work*, she thought, picking up another application.

Jenna worked a few extra shifts at the diner that week

to make some extra money. She never made much on tips, nor did she expect to make more than fifty a week from the crowd that came into the place. *Just a stepping stone*, Jenna kept telling herself. *It certainly can't get worse than this.*

Letting her mind wander as she filled drinks and delivered food for the patrons at the diner, she thrust her chin forward and pushed aside all thoughts of her financial predicament. A distinct image immediately replaced the formerly negative thoughts: one of David Langley's coppery eyes and half-smirk as he was seated at the bar of the diner. Jenna sighed.

She hadn't been able to keep his image out of her head since. Thoughts of David Langley's powerful arms and commanding presence always found their way into her dreams. Often it was the accident, but even that would get her heart thumping all over again. She remembered how he'd looked in the hospital, beaten and broken, and then how thoroughly composed he'd been at the diner. He spoke to her with such ease that day, as if time was no obstacle. The confidence of cops had always bothered Jenna; in her experience, such confidence often stemmed from arrogance. But Mr. David Langley was causing her to doubt her convictions against them all, and that frankly terrified her.

Shaking her head, she forced herself to focus on more pressing matters. She'd put in the last of the job applications that week and was hoping for a callback soon. Unbeknownst to her brother, she had replaced the cell phone she'd chucked earlier in the month and had put her new number on all of the job applications. The last thing she needed was her brother fielding calls from her potential employers from his house phone.

Jenna drove her Datsun back to her brother's house. It was barely one o'clock in the afternoon, sun high in the sky.

She'd gotten off about three hours early from the diner. The day had been a complete drag and since she'd worked the most so far that week, she was sent home for the day. She saw her brother's car parked in the driveway and the garage door open as she pulled up. As she parked and slammed her car door, she heard murmurings coming from within the shadows of the garage.

Walking up the driveway, she decided to head for the front door instead of going through the group of men she saw gathered around the motorcycles lined up in the two car stall.

As she put her key in the lock, she heard one of them bark. "Who's that?"

"Jenna!" Her brother yelled.

"Yeah Frankie, it's me."

"Come here a minute."

She heard someone slam the garage door that led to the inside of the house. Her brother Frank was standing over his bike, a beer in one hand. He was a large man both in height and size. Frank had a bandana tied around his head and a leather vest over a red t-shirt. His jeans were filthy and his tall black boots were covered in dust.

Frank turned to stare at Jenna. His eyes were the same color as hers, a misty blue. He sported a blonde mustache and a buzz cut under the bandana. He'd gotten into a lot of trouble as a teen after their father's abuse at the hands of Brookside PD: some vandalism, stolen cars and drug possession. Frank loved the bad boy persona and had embraced it fully by age 16. He bought a low-riding motorcycle as soon as he landed a construction job when he was 19. Although he always preached to Jenna about outgrowing his teenage rebellion, he still had a rap sheet that followed him everywhere.

Jenna loved her brother; after the death of their mother during the traumatic trial process and their father's troubled life after his exoneration, her brother was all Jenna truly had left. He had been the only one to help her through her entire recovery after she'd been injured. He'd been the one to save her from herself, bringing her back to reality after the emotional damage of an abrupt end to her promising military career. Jenna was eternally grateful for his commitment to her; he had given her a new perspective on life by encouraging Jenna to embrace an uncertain future instead of dwelling on a past that could not be changed.

But in the past six months, Frank had started acting strangely. Jenna assumed her dependency on him had gone to his head. He'd done nothing but try to micromanage every aspect of her life ever since. Where are you going, who are you hanging out with, why don't you tell me when you're leaving? Jenna took it in stride as best she could, considering it her burden to bear in payment for his sacrifice to her. *He's only looking out after my best interests*, Jenna told herself.

"Jenna, this is my buddy Rick."

"Hello, Rick." She took the squat man's hand in her own. His beefy hand squeezed exceptionally hard over hers, and she forced her lips into a smile.

"We've got some stuff to do inside real quick, it should only be a minute."

"No problem Frank."

Jenna went to wait outside, but her eyes caught on something stuck in her brother's waistband, a glint of metal. Before she could get a good look, Frank pulled his shirt down, turning away.

But to her, it had looked like the butt of a gun, which she knew her brother wasn't allowed to legally own or possess.

Thoughts raced through her head, but she came up with no answers. Besides, she hadn't actually *seen* anything. It could have just been his belt buckle...

Jenna knew better. *And what can you do about it, Jenna?*

She felt fear grip her, a sudden tightness in her chest. Her brother had insisted on being a law-abiding citizen for the past six years: holding a job, renting a house, being responsible in life. Now all of that was coming into question for Jenna. If he was putting on a front, he was doing quite a fine job of it.

"Alright Jenna, you're good." He called from the garage.

She expeditiously made her way through the door and up to her little room. Shutting the door behind her, she scanned her room to make sure nothing was out of place. Not that there was much of hers to move. It all seemed to be in order, just as she'd left it earlier that morning.

"I need a drink," Jenna grumbled to herself. She'd been working her ass off every day trying to find another job and tip-toeing around her brother. She was going to follow up on some of the applications, and then she was going to go out and treat herself for once.

As she started to get herself ready, she turned on the TV to listen to the news.

CHAPTER NINE

LANGLEY FELT GOOD. The day was young and his team had finally made a break in one of their smaller cases. They were making a mad dash around the office, grabbing up the paperwork they had on one Marco Valdez. A patrol officer had just happened to pull Marco over at an apartment complex on the more criminally-inclined side of town earlier in the morning. Not realizing who he was, the officer had released him and was then instructed by Langley's unit to back off. The department's eye in the sky was able to keep track and told them what apartment he'd entered.

It took a half hour to get the judge to sign the search warrant. Miller had attempted to assign Langley to the desks, to which Langley replied with a raucous protest, practically begging to be included on the raid. They came to an agreement that Langley would stay with Miller, fielding radios and phone calls while the other detectives handled the dirty work. Langley was happily geared up and ready to go with Greer, Barnes and Neil, a behemoth of a detective that had been working the unit for under a year.

Lieutenant Miller came barging into the room, fax in hand.

"We got it. Let's roll."

They piled into two police SUVs and high tailed it over to the apartment complex.

It was a lovely afternoon. A few birds were chirping in the trees, a couple was pushing their baby in a stroller and a few teenage boys were playing basketball in the street. Thankfully, Marco was in a downstairs apartment. However, they had no idea who else might be in there with him.

They had been trying to find Marco's operating house for months now. It was amazing how these things worked—simply not using his turn signal had started his downfall today.

The four detectives drew their weapons; Miller scanned the street with his back to his team. Langley and Barnes stood off to the side while Neil banged loudly on the door.

"Brookside Police Department!"

Nothing.

"Brookside Police, open the door!"

They heard a crash inside the apartment. No one was going to come to the door, and they all knew it.

Neil tried the door and chuckled as he turned the unlocked knob, throwing the door wide with a gentle push of his hand. He slipped inside with his pistol level, clearing the first room with Greer.

"Guy on the couch!" Greer called out as the two of them continued towards the back of the apartment. Barnes and Langley went into the first room and Barnes immediately went over to the obese man lying on the couch. She grabbed his wrist, then stuck her fingers into his fat neck. There was a swarm of flies hovering just above the couch as Barnes poked and prodded. The stench of sweat, drugs and filth filled Langley's nostrils, making him grimace.

"I can't find a pulse on this guy. He's not breathing."

"Dead guy on the couch," Langley called out.

"Clear!" Greer called as they exited a room.

Then they heard a shriek from the last bedroom. Marco Valdez, clothed only in a pair of red underwear, came screaming down the hallway, hands over his head as if he were on fire.

Neil flew into him, smashing him against the wall. A few pictures rattled and fell to the ground, bouncing around Neil's feet. Naked Marco was screaming like a banshee as they crashed to the floor in a heap of tangled limbs. Marco was squirming on the carpet under Neil's bulk.

Greer grabbed a flailing arm, but the man was slick with sweat and he easily pulled away. Langley glanced at the front door and motioned for Barnes to go help.

"Jesus! Dude, calm down!" Greer growled. The man continued to wail as three detectives piled on top of him. Langley knew he would only get in the way in the cramped hallway, so he started canvassing the kitchen.

On the dining room table—more accurately, a card table that was approximately twenty years old—were ten bricks of marijuana, a couple crack pipes, and a large pile of white pills that looked like PCP or acid.

Lieutenant Miller stood outside the door, hands on his hips.

"You might want to get the coroner and an officer escort," Langley pointed a thumb over his shoulder at the nearly naked man that was still putting up a raucous fight.

Miller nodded, pulling his cell out of his pocket. As he dialed, he took a few shuffling steps to stand inside the doorway beside the table, his back to Langley as he kept a watch outside.

Langley holstered his weapon as they finally clicked the first handcuff on the screaming man, still writhing on the floor. Greer was sitting on him like he would a horse; Barnes was holding his legs and Neil was kneeling on his shoulders while finishing up with the handcuffs. Langley started calculating the street cost of the drugs while swatting flies from his face.

"SAAAAALAAA!"

"Wha—Aaah!" Langley cried out as the dead guy on the couch roared to life and covered the ground between them in one stride. Before Langley could even turn, the fat behemoth grabbed Langley into a flying bear hug, pinning his arms tight to his sides.

Langley's feet left the ground and the two men came crashing down onto the crusty floor, Langley crushed underneath the copious bulk of the man.

"Langley!" Lieutenant Miller shrieked, dropping his phone. Miller dove on top of the fat man and tried to drag him off by a beefy leg.

Langley squirmed, trying to catch a breath as he kneed the man in the groin. As if it had no effect, the man screamed in Langley's face, flashing teeth that hadn't been brushed in at least a year.

And then Greer was there, taser in hand.

"Don't...miss..." Langley grunted as he struggled with the man trying to strangle him.

He missed.

Langley's body locked up and he screamed for the whole five second ride of pure agony. The fat man was also shrieking into Langley's face and convulsing on top of him.

Greer and Miller rolled the man off of Langley and Barnes pulled the taser prong from Langley's arm, tossing it over her shoulder. Greer slammed the taser against the formerly dead guy's back, giving him another round without Langley being part of the circuit.

"Oh God, Langley. Are you okay?"

Langley curled up into the fetal position on the floor, his ribs aflame. He couldn't breathe and the room was spinning wildly.

"*Fuck!*" Lieutenant Miller barked. Two pairs of cuffs and zip-ties were swiftly put on the fat man and he lay on the floor a few feet from Langley, blubbering to himself.

Langley groaned, clutching his side with one hand as he panted. He grabbed his face with his other hand, gripping his own forehead with clenched fingertips.

Barnes had her hand on his shoulder. Greer and Miller had the fat man, Neil held naked Marco.

"Fuck!" Miller repeated. The Lieutenant started calling for more back up officers to help expedite the process. Greer towed the fat man outside and Neil half carried the shrill naked guy out behind him.

"Langley. Langley! *David!*"

Langley forced his eyes open, still holding his ribs. If they had been cracked before, they now felt shattered. Though the effects of the torturous taser had immediately worn off, the lasting damage of a three hundred pound man landing on him was still making Langley's efforts to breathe extremely difficult.

"AMR is en route." Miller said, kneeling over Langley. Langley felt a rough hand grab his arm. "Are you okay?"

"No," Langley mumbled into his hand.

Miller talked into his hand-held radio as other officers started arriving. Someone was snapping pictures of the drugs, others were marking evidence and cordoning off the area. Barnes stayed perched protectively over Langley, shooing away the beat cops that tried to ask questions as to why there was a detective splayed on the ground, cluttering up the middle of the scene. He vaguely heard someone ask if he'd been the one to get hit by a car, and Barnes answered hostilely, silencing the street cops once and for all.

Langley lethargically waved Miller and Barnes away from him as he took his time to sit upright.

His head was throbbing, his side a constant stabbing pain. Langley closed his eyes to steady himself as he sat on the floor, legs stretched out in front of him. He clutched his side with one hand and the other stayed on the floor to balance him until the room stopped spinning.

He opened his eyes as he heard Greer's voice.

"Langley! Sorry man—"

"I'm going to punch...you in the face." Langley took small breaths to prevent his ribs from hurting any more than they already did.

"I deserve that, and more." Greer extended his hand and Langley carefully took it. Greer slowly pulled Langley to his feet and Langley immediately doubled over, gritting his teeth.

"I just got...raped...by a grizzly bear." Langley muttered.

"Of all the goddamn people, Langley," Miller said as he paced the tiny living room. "That guy ran right by me to get to you."

"Well, that was the first time I've ever tased two people at once," Greer said jovially, as if it were an accomplishment.

"And *dammit* Barnes, do I need to explain what 'dead' means? You are indefinitely banned from dead-checking, am I clear?" Miller waved his arms animatedly as he glared at Barnes. Langley watched her nod once, then saw her roll her eyes when Miller turned away.

The stench of the room finally hit Langley and he felt himself involuntarily heave. He stopped it from coming up at great cost to his ribs; Greer grabbed him, trying to avoid Langley's numerous injuries and half-carried, half-dragged him out of the apartment.

Miller had retrieved his phone and was making calls while managing the radio traffic; Barnes was helping some of the officers at the scene.

A media truck had already arrived and the blubbering obese man was sobbing into the cameras from the back of the police car. Miller growled loudly, shooing the reporters away as they dragged Langley towards the ambulance. Miller yelled at a beat cop for leaving the windows down as Langley heard the fat man screaming "I'm innocent! I was just a bystander!" Greer shook his head, holding Langley upright.

"Yeah, right. Tackled and tried to strangle a cop. Real innocent!"

Neil finished loading up the naked guy and was making his way towards Greer and Langley.

"Good work, team!" Neil fist-pumped the air as if his favorite football team had just won the Super Bowl.

"Go screw yourself, Neil." Langley grimaced. Greer laughed heartily.

"Hit with a car, tackled by a dead man the size of a fridge and tased by your partner," Greer was counting on his free hand. "I think you deserve a beer."

They dragged Langley towards the awaiting ambulance.

"I'll be fine," Langley grumbled in protest.

Greer shook his head. "Protocol, man. Get checked and then we can roll."

The paramedic was kind enough to reset a few ribs that

had shifted slightly out of place during the tackle. Exhausted and sore, Langley leaned heavily on the ambulance until Greer pulled up the SUV.

Barnes helped Langley crawl into the backseat. Langley laid down across the bench, covering his head with his hands as he focused on breathing in slow, calm breaths. He knew he looked utterly pathetic, and he didn't give a damn. The engine sputtered before starting and Langley's entire side went numb. Barnes climbed in the passenger seat.

"LT says to take care of Langley first and that we've got to have our reports in by tomorrow night," Greer announced. Langley grunted acknowledgment as Greer turned the car. One word answers were tolerable; anything more was torture on the rib cage.

"Langley," Greer's voice was tense.

"Mmm."

"You want to go to the hospital, man?"

"No."

A moment of silence.

"Seriously. I owe you a lot of beer for tasing you."

"Yeah."

"If you're up to it, I'll meet you at Duke's tonight and buy you as many rounds as you want."

"Yes."

"Barnes?"

"I'm down."

"Right on."

When they arrived at the police station, Langley told Greer to grab his truck keys. Driving would be far too painful. And now just the act of standing upright was excruciating. Barnes was going to get started on the clean-up paperwork with Neil but agreed to drive her car behind them so Greer could go back and finish up his own work at the station. Greer hopped into Langley's driver's seat and drove Langley to his apartment.

"See you in a few hours, Langley." Greer parked the truck and tossed Langley the keys. Barnes honked as they pulled away, leaving Langley at his door.

Langley staggered into the bathroom and started a hot shower. He let the water run over him, trying to forget the past four hours, and hoping the next four would make up for it.

CHAPTER TEN

LANGLEY WAS FULLY EMBRACING the pity-party he was throwing himself in the corner of the bar as he waited for Greer and Barnes. He quietly brooded over his barely-touched beer and glazed over the football game that was happening on the TV behind the counter. The drive over had been hell enough and sitting in a bar stool was wreaking havoc on his rib cage as he had to keep twisting to stay in his seat.

In mild terms, Langley was fucking *miserable*. Nothing in the Marine Corps or the police department had ever compared to the nonstop physical pain he was enduring right now. The only thing that kept him from downright sobbing on the bar was the replaying of the phone conversation he'd had with Jenna. *She offered to buy me breakfast*, Langley reminisced. He took a swig of his beer, remembering the stutter in her delicate voice. He wondered when he might have the chance to see her again, to rest his eyes upon her soft, sensual lips and her freckled cheeks.

He heard a bar stool abruptly skitter across the floor as he took another sip of his drink, but couldn't turn himself around fast enough to identify where it was happening.

"Take it easy, darlin!"

"You, you *weasel*! Get away from me!"

Langley choked on his beer as he identified the source of the ruckus. He rose a bit too quickly and had to brace himself on the wall. There, standing at the table, was Jenna; she was berating a drunk in a cowboy hat and had knocked her bar stool over in the process.

With a sudden flutter in his step, Langley closed the distance between them and put a hand on the weasel's shoulder as he set his own beer on her table, silently thanking the man for providing the most amazing opportunity for him.

"Is this man bothering you?" Langley asked, admiring Jenna's flushed face and pursed lips.

When her eyes met Langley's, Langley held his breath. A look of shock was quickly replaced by barely-controlled hostility on Jenna's delicate features. Langley was genuinely surprised by the anger in her glare.

"You," Jenna pointed a finger at Langley. The weasel, realizing he was no longer the recipient of Jenna's ferocity, quickly fled the scene. Jenna stayed silent, sneering at Langley as if she couldn't quite string words together.

Langley cocked his head sideways and lifted his hands in surrender. "Did I miss something?"

Jenna's nose crinkled when she uttered something about cops that Langley didn't catch. Langley turned his palms upward while furrowing his brow at her sudden disdain. *Is this the same Jenna that wanted to buy me breakfast?*

"I'm confused."

Jenna took a moment and huffed, lips quivering. She retrieved her bar stool and sat down, leaning back and crossing her arms as she glared in every direction.

Langley couldn't help but notice the now-accentuated cleavage under her gray sweater; it was the sweater she'd worn the day of the wreck, Langley realized. The sudden realization made him get light-headed as he involuntarily envisioned headlights.

He leaned hard on the table, suddenly out of air.

"Are you going to faint?" Jenna asked, not politely.

Langley floundered for a stool. "Possibly." He sat down hard, causing a shock of pain to his ribs.

Jenna was coldly silent as he took the time to regulate his breathing. The room finally stopped spinning and Langley rested his eyes on her again, absorbing her angry passion. She seemed to be fighting some demon inside herself; her face was a battleground of anger, pity and regret. Langley couldn't help but notice, it was what the past ten years of Marine Corps and police work had taught him to do, absorb every emotion from a person. But even though he could identify what was going on by her subtle expressions, he still had no idea what on earth was causing her to feel those emotions.

"What happened to you?" Jenna asked him quietly.

Langley couldn't stop the small laugh that escaped his throat. He wanted to shout out of frustration, but instead he regarded Jenna coolly.

"Could you be a little more specific?"

Jenna was in no mood for humor as her nostrils flared. *What have I done to deserve this?* Langley waited patiently for a response nonetheless.

"I saw on the news what you and your team did to that man today at the fifth street apartments." Jenna's eyebrows shot up as she spoke. "I saw you in the background." She looked at something to her left. "And I saw the bystander that was roughed up by your team. Is that what you do? Use your badge to intimidate people and take out your rage on them?" Langley was too stunned to speak. "I thought, before, that you were different. But what you did today tells me you're just as arrogant and corrupt as the rest of them." She was gripping her own shoulders with her hands as she turned back to look at Langley with open hostility.

Langley was utterly taken aback. Not only was he having the shittiest day ever (well, aside from the day spent getting hit by a car), but now the only thing, the only person that had been holding him together was chastising him like a petulant child, prejudging him, hitting him emotionally where it hurt the most. Langley wanted to both scream in anger and cry from the pathetic irony of it all. *It always comes down to assuming abuse of the badge. Not every cop is an asshole, woman!* He loathed having to defend his honor, especially to people with misperceptions and preconceived notions, and her accusatory words were enough to trigger him, flaming a fury within him that Langley hadn't felt in a long time.

"Holy hell. I don't recall you being there, yet you act like you know what happened based on a short news clip! Do you have *any* interest in hearing the truth, or are you convinced you already know it? Let me know so I can save my breath for someone who *gives a damn*," Langley suddenly barked as he slid his arms onto the table, causing Jenna to lean back even further, her eyes wide. He put a pointed, shaking finger to his temple and tapped slowly. "Are you aware that people—and the media—*lie* to discredit us because it makes for a better story than the facts?"

Jenna sneered at him but Langley did not back down; he emitted a snarl as he banged his hand on the bar, sending his beer hopping sideways. Jenna flinched, her eyes squeezing shut for a brief moment. *Damn her for provoking me*, he fumed. He quickly regained control of himself, angry that he'd gone on a tirade that now had his side cramping painfully.

Her lip quivered. She took a deep, shaky breath. But she remained quiet as she lifted her chin, revealing a slender neck. Langley accepted her angry silence as permission for him to speak.

As he took a calming breath, his cell phone rang.

Jenna was struggling between wanting to believe that David Langley was different than the cops that beat her father, the cops that flexed their muscles and flashed their badges to exert power over the weak. But she was having a difficult time trying to balance the resentment she harbored towards the badge and the overwhelming desire to keep watching his ears redden with rage as he passionately defended his honor.

She could tell he was hurting the instant he'd arrived at her table, but his sudden and unrepressed ferocity unnerved Jenna when she'd confronted him. When he slammed his hand on the table, Jenna was legitimately frightened he might completely lose it, and Jenna wasn't sure what might happen if he did. But he'd shut down his fury in the next moment, his breathing steady as his fiery eyes continued to gleam.

As he went to explain, his phone rang.

He glanced at it before answering. "Langley."

Jenna could only hear the tone of a man's voice. Langley rested his head in his hand and rubbed his forehead before speaking. He took a deep breath.

"It's fine, don't worry about it. But before you go, can you do me a quick favor?" Langley put the phone down onto the table and pressed the speaker button. He pushed it with one finger until it rested in the middle of the table. Jenna gingerly set her arms on the table so that she could be in ear shot of the phone, realizing he was doing it for her benefit.

"Of course, man, anything." The man's voice was clear and crisp.

"Can you give my friend here a quick, civilian-rated breakdown on how my day has been?" The way he said 'friend' made Jenna's heart skip a beat.

There was a bark on the other end of the phone and some scuffling. "Are they aware you got hit by a car?"

"Yes."

"Well then, today's menu included getting tackled by a three hundred pound formerly dead guy," there was a pause, and then a female's voice was on the line.

"And then getting trounced and strangled on the floor by said dead guy."

"And then I inadvertently tased you, along with the dead guy that was trying to kill you."

"All of which scored you some extra dislocated ribs, if I remember correctly," the woman continued. Jenna couldn't bring herself to look away from the phone during the lull in the speech. Her cheeks instantly heated. *Oh God, there's no way he's going to forgive me for what I said.*

"And I think that sums it up, right?" It was the man again.

"Yep, good enough. Thank you." Langley took the phone off speaker and listened to the man before replying. "Seriously, don't worry about it. See you tomorrow."

He hung up the phone, eyes lingering on his beer as he tapped the bottom of it gently on the table with both hands.

"I'm such an ass," Jenna groaned, resting her face in her hands. "David, I—" but she stuttered into silence when warm hands embraced hers, pulling them away from her face. His hands were rough but gentle; as he held her outstretched hands over the table, he looked into her eyes.

Jenna was rendered immobile by the deep coppery hues that seemed to dance in the dim lighting. One corner of his mouth twitched upwards, sending a shiver down Jenna's spine.

"So, how was your day today, Jenna?" His voice was barely audible, more gruff than normal.

"I'm so sorry," Jenna stuttered, feeling terrible. Seeing the pain in his face over her accusations made her eyes sting with sudden tears.

"Sorry if I scared you."

Jenna shook her head slightly, "I offended you." He dipped his head down once in a curt nod as she watched his tongue drag along the inside of his mouth. Jenna stared at him as he suddenly canted his head to the side, his eyes focused on Jenna's left hand.

He took her hand and slowly lifted it up off the table, examining her wrist. Confused, Jenna watched him turn her arm under the light. He caressed her wrist with his fingers and rubbed his thumb in a small circle, a smirk on his face.

"What?" Jenna frowned.

The smirk broke into a full, secretive smile, one that made Jenna instantly melt inside. *He defies everything I've ever believed about cops.*

"It's nothing," David said, bringing her hand up to his mouth. As he kissed her wrist, Jenna's legs trembled. His lips were tender, moist. Jenna's mouth suddenly went dry as he released her hands and braced himself against the table.

"Thank you," he whispered.

"Thank *me?*" Jenna put a hand to her chest. "For what?"

"For turning the two worst days of my life into the best two days of my life."

He went to get up from the table, but grabbed his side with a grimace.

Jenna couldn't fly off of her bar stool fast enough. She was immediately beside him, putting her shoulder underneath his arm.

She caught a whiff of his scent, a wonderful blend of cedar and citrus. Imagining him using such soap over his muscled physique nearly made her knees buckle.

As he leaned on Jenna's shoulder, they clasped their hands together to help brace him as he walked. Jenna wrapped her other arm around his side, careful to avoid the injured ribs as she helped guide him towards the exit. His back was taut as he took slow steps; her hand brushed into a small, holstered weapon on his side as they weaved through the patrons at the bar.

Jenna basked in his warmth, cherishing the feeling of his strong arm around her shoulders. He was doing his best to compose himself, but Jenna could tell he was not doing well at all.

"You can't drive in your condition," Jenna said as she opened the door of the bar and shuffled outside with Langley. She expected an argument, but instead he just smirked slightly as he glanced down at her face.

"Jenna, ever my rescuer." He leaned his head over to put his nose and lips against the top of her head. The gesture made Jenna tingle all over. She had to stop herself from begging him to say her name again.

"I'll drive you home," Jenna told him as they made their way through the brisk, dimly lit parking lot. Langley's breathing was raspy, but he was clinging to some of his dignity and was putting on a very convincing face of tranquility. He didn't protest, but instead allowed himself to be led by Jenna.

She stopped in front of her car and dug in her pocket to get out her keys.

"Nice car," he said, eyeing her Datsun. He rested his hand on the roof as Jenna unlocked the passenger door. She opened it for him, then grabbed him under the arms to help him as he began to lower himself into the cramped seat. His back was solid against her hands.

She quickly shut the passenger door and hopped into the driver's seat.

*Oh Lord, if my father or brother saw this...*Jenna jammed the key in and the car roared to life.

Langley had certainly not expected this outcome, but he knew that Jenna was right. Whatever was causing the acute pain in his side would make driving a hazard for everyone on the road. He was quiet during the drive, trying to focus his eyes out the window instead of staring at Jenna. He offered brief directions until they arrived at his apartment complex.

A sudden feeling of embarrassment washed over him. He wondered if she owned a house, if she'd be ashamed of his ramshackle little place he called home. *Too late now*.

"David, what happened to your cane?"

Langley chuckled as he slowly extracted himself from her car.

"I shot it."

Jenna snorted. It was an endearing sound to Langley's ears. Then, as Jenna offered a shoulder to lean on, she let out a loud groan.

"I should have known."

"What?"

"Of course. You were a Marine, weren't you." It wasn't a question. She looked up at him with big blue eyes and emitted a sigh of exasperation.

He couldn't help the smile that crossed his lips. "What gave you that idea?"

They stopped at his door. He fished for his keys while eyeing Jenna sideways.

"Are you kidding?" Jenna waved her arms, conducting an imaginary orchestra. "You *scream* Marine." She started counting animatedly with both hands. "Hit by a car helping a fellow brother-in-arms, stalking girls at restaurants, shooting inanimate objects not designed to be shot at and going to the bar instead of the hospital, which is where you should be right now. Tell me that is *not* the textbook definition of a Marine."

Langley roared with laughter, embracing the pain of the act. "Well damn if you don't have me pegged." He pushed open his door, and the action made his side go numb in a very disconcerting way.

"Are you sure you're okay? You look like you're going to puke."

"It's fine." He stayed in his doorway.

Jenna frowned at him. She closed the gap between them with one step and brusquely moved Langley's arms away from his sides so that she could place her hands on his rib cage. Langley flinched but a hard glare from Jenna made him stop his attempt to pull away.

"Liar."

It was the first time in his life that such an accusation fell pleasantly on his ears. Langley stood there as she rubbed her hands slowly along his sides. Even through the waves of pain, the inevitable reaction to Jenna's delicate hands rubbing on his torso took hold. He tried to turn to cover the sudden rise in his jeans.

"Stand still." She barked, all business.

She reached his hips, then traced her hands back up and around him so that she was feeling along his back. Her breasts were now alarming close and he had a fantastic view straight down her gray sweater—the sweater that Langley had earlier noticed was still ever-so-lightly stained by a stubborn smudge of his blood from the wreck. The lacy black bra was just visible beyond the curve of her breasts.

Langley sucked in air as her delicate hands ran over his quivering muscles. A small moan escaped his lips.

Her hands suddenly stopped.

"David."

"What?"

"Your floating rib is subluxated."

"What the hell does that mean?"

Jenna sounded exasperated. "It means you need to go to the hospital."

Langley shook his head. "Not going to happen."

"You need to get it reset. Get back in the car."

He waved his hand and took a step into his apartment. A firm hand grabbed his forearm, causing him to twist in a way he wasn't expecting. He yelped.

"Sorry!" Jenna immediately withdrew her hand. However, sympathy vacated her features immediately and was replaced with the most obvious 'I-told-you-so' look. "See? Hospital. Now."

Langley waved a hand dismissively. "I'll deal with it tomorrow."

"No! The longer you wait the more likely it is to slip again later." She crossed her arms over her chest, her blue eyes narrowed.

"If it's that urgent, why don't you just fix it then?"

"I am not going to be responsible for puncturing your lung, or something worse."

"Fine. Thanks for driving me home. " Langley reached carefully for his door knob.

She slapped the door back open. They stood motionless, blinking at one another. She finally caved. "I can't believe I'm actually agreeing to this."

Langley flashed his best, cheesiest grin. He stepped all the way inside his apartment and held open the door for her.

But before Jenna stepped over the threshold, she froze. Her eyes suddenly glazed over, her breath stuck in her throat. Langley had seen that absent look many times before; it was the blank expression that often overtook someone when they were reliving their own personal nightmares. Langley frowned. *What trauma have I managed to dredge up by opening my door?*

Langley didn't have an answer yet, but his investigative mind was now on heightened alert. She tried to cover her pause by tussling with her hair before taking the step across the threshold.

What's going on in that head of yours, Jenna?

CHAPTER ELEVEN

JENNA WAS CERTAIN LANGLEY could hear her heart thumping as she crossed over that boundary between the outside world and the inside of his apartment. She felt as if she were walking into a prison cell, a place where she was betraying her father, her family, her mother's memories and everything that had transpired a decade ago. She felt dishonorable, ashamed; she could not accept that she was falling so hard for a *cop*. *And yet, here you are.* Jenna felt a part of her go selectively numb with disbelief; it was the only way for her to lessen the guilt of her treachery. She blocked out the welling emotions, both reasonable and unreasonable, and the only feeling left was a fear of the unknown.

Jenna blinked rapidly, clearing her thoughts. The apartment was practically barren. An old couch, a coffee table. Counters clean, no dining table. A few small plaques hung on the wall, most of them Marine Corps related. There was one photo of a young David Langley smiling with another man, both of them in folding chairs with a number of stringed instruments all around them.

Langley shut the door and was attempting to take off

his boots.

"Here," Jenna dropped to her knee and wrapped a hand around his ankle.

"I can do—"

"Shut it, David." She pulled off his weathered boots one at a time.

He inhaled sharply, but when she looked up she saw a flash of white teeth beneath his smirk. "Thank you." He offered her a hand up and she stood, facing him, her eyes level with his broad shoulders. *He's the opposite of the alpha I keep expecting*, Jenna mused. *Always willing to concede.*

"I need you to sit down," Jenna was doing her best to keep herself composed, but being in his presence was making her lose her ability to reason.

He gestured to the open doorway.

Oh Lord, the bedroom. She quickly shucked her boots and left them right next to the closed front door, her only avenue of escape.

David walked ahead of her, his chiseled arms hanging loosely at his sides. He removed his belt in a swift motion and set his holstered revolver on the empty nightstand next to his immaculately made bed.

His closet was half-open and Jenna peeked inside as she turned the corner. There were two pairs of perfectly polished boots, a set of inspection-ready dress blues with numerous rows of ribbons in perfect order. A glint of light reflected off the crossed rifle and pistol expert badges.

There was a TV on a dresser and the only thing visible on the far side of the bed was an old folding chair and a— *what the hell was that? A cello?*

Jenna felt a wave of heat wash over her as she scanned the room. *I don't belong here.*

He cleared his throat, making Jenna jump. She cleared

her throat in response, her legs suddenly weak.

"Sit down," she ordered.

He obeyed.

Jenna felt herself floating towards the bed. She put her hand under his elbow and lifted his arm. He allowed himself to be maneuvered; his eyes were glassy and disengaged as he focused on something directly in front of him. Jenna crossed his arm over his chest and then leaned over to grab his other arm.

Her chest brushed his elbow, making her recoil. Langley seemed oblivious; his steady gaze never wavered. His lack of response made Jenna wonder if only she was feeling the overwhelming sparks of sensuality.

She placed his other arm across his body so that he was hugging himself.

"Try to relax."

Jenna was shaking as she lifted her hands. *You're a corpsman. Snap out of it. Just relocate the damn rib.*

"I, um, have to—"

"Do whatever you have to do, Jenna."

She felt her belly surge with warmth as he said her name. She took a deep breath, then wrapped her arms around his torso, feeling his rock solid muscles flex beneath her touch.

Jenna closed her eyes to try and focus, but Langley's warm breath was tickling her neck. She was acutely aware how close her breasts were to his chest, how warm his body was against hers.

She felt along his back, then placed her fist carefully on the rib that was out of place. Gently, she pushed and guided him with her shoulder as she kept her fist steady. Following her lead, he slowly sank back on his bed, Jenna's arms beneath him as he laid himself down flat. Jenna nimbly climbed atop him, being extremely careful to keep her body as far away from his as possible while she worked. She placed one foot on the bed near his hip to brace herself while her other knee came dangerously close to making contact between his legs.

Jenna could not stop herself from glancing down as she refined her position above him, hugging him tightly while applying pressure on his rib with her fist. His jeans were *much* tighter in that region than she formerly remembered. Looking at David's barely contained erection caused a slew of involuntary physical reactions that made Jenna start to sweat.

Do not screw this up, Jenna chastised herself. She looked back to David's face. His eyes were closed, his eyebrows betraying just how much he was hurting even though his breathing was regular. There was a single bead of sweat hovering near the scar above his ear.

"Take deep breaths," Jenna said hoarsely. Feeling his body moving rhythmically beneath her practically made her scream aloud. She wanted him. Wanted him so badly at that moment that she was nearly to orgasm just thinking about it. Then the responding, overwhelming fear of betraying her family made her whole body tremble with anguish.

Her rational brain quickly replaced those thoughts with the terrifying notion that if she failed to properly reset his rib, she would not only make an ass out of herself but could also seriously damage his internal organs in the process.

It was a lot to process.

After his fourth breath, Jenna lifted up with her fist and jolted herself down—hard—onto his torso, leveraging the rib. She was rewarded with an audible pop.

Langley grunted, opening his eyes.

Jenna quickly withdrew her hands out from under him. "Did I hurt you?"

"Mmmm. No." Langley whispered.

Jenna couldn't bring herself to move. She was still above him, her knee positioned between his legs. She was trying to make the split-second decision between leaping off the bed away from him or—*stop this now, Jenna, or you'll lose yourself.*

Langley made the decision for her. Much quicker than Jenna expected, Langley sat upright, meeting her chest-to-chest as she slid both her legs down and stood on the ground, her stomach brushing against his hard torso as she leaned against the bed. His groin made contact with her thigh and Jenna shivered, but he kept her momentum going and pushed her back a step so that there was space between them.

He enveloped her hands within his and looked down. The motion was friendly, warm.

"Jenna," he said as his eyes slowly worked their way up until they met with hers once again. His copper eyes were sharp, focused only on her face as he sat on the edge of his bed. "How can I ever thank y—"

Jenna couldn't take it any longer. She cupped both sides of his face in her hands and crushed her lips against his.

The shock of her wet lips against his made Langley moan aloud. His cock was practically ripping his jeans apart as she held his face to hers, her tongue darting into his mouth.

A high-pitched whine escaped his lips as Jenna took in a breath. He ran his hands up her tight thighs and rested them on her narrow waist. He had never wanted a woman more, and it took serious focus to resist ripping her clothes off and taking her right then and there. And Langley was keenly aware that she was far more than just merely willing to do the same.

Yet, as she backed away from the kiss, Langley immediately sensed a subtle darkness take over her. Her nostrils flared and her jaw clenched as she glanced at something above Langley's head. Although he could tell that she was just as physically aroused as he was with her pebbled nipples and flushed cheeks, her mind was still subconsciously battling some demon Langley had yet to identify. The slight tension in her shoulders, the sudden gritting of her teeth, a flash of...anguish? Regret? Something was happening that was making her mentally resist what she was doing with him, whether she realized it or not.

His body was screaming to caress those perky tits, squeeze her ass as she mounted and enveloped the length of him. Langley practically came at the thought.

But the last thing Langley wanted was for her to regret the decisions she made here tonight. And he knew from his own experience that if she went all the way with him right now, she was going to create a connection between her demons and *him*.

Langley did not want to be her fling; he would not be a sex object for a regrettable one night stand. No, he wanted more than that. He wanted her to give herself over to him, heart and soul. Forever. He had never wanted that in any other woman before now.

And that meant doing the hardest fucking thing he'd ever done in his life.

Before she could descend upon him for another kiss, Langley grasped her hips firmly; he carefully applied enough pressure so that she took a tiny step back.

Forcing her body those few scant inches away, even though Langley knew it was for her benefit alone, was ripping his heart out. And he knew it was only going to get harder.

"Jenna," he whispered hoarsely. "You don't have to do this right now."

Her mouth dropped open. "Are...are you kidding me?"

Langley rubbed his face with his hand, ignoring the throb in his jeans. "Is there something you want to talk about?"

Jenna turned crimson, her voice trembling. "Talk? No, I don't want to *talk*." She clenched her fists, flexing all the muscles in her arms as she snarled. "What the hell is this, a therapy session?"

"No," Langley said calmly, his cock still pulsating as Jenna began panting. "I'm getting the feeling you're not telling me something."

She was immobile for two seconds before utterly losing it.

"You are either the *densest* man on the planet, or you're a tremendous asshole."

Langley stood up carefully, hands open in front of him. He had expected the anger and the insults; that was normal considering he'd just embarrassed the hell out of her.

"Jenna, I don't want anything to happen right now that you're not mentally prepared for."

Her response was a shrill laugh. "If I didn't want to do this, I wouldn't be here right now!" She shook her head as tears sprang to her eyes. "Who the hell do you think you are?"

Sure, it was easy in an interrogation room to emotionally arouse a suspect to motivate the truth to come forth. But doing it to someone you loved—*wait, sweet mercy, do I actually love her?*

A tear fell and she tried to hurriedly wipe it away. Langley desperately wanted to wrap his arms around her and let his body absorb her tears, but he knew he couldn't approach her right now. Testing the waters, he subconsciously reached a hand towards her. As he expected, she recoiled like a pissed-off cat ready to strike.

"Don't you dare." She hissed.

"Jenna," Langley whispered, blinking away the sudden sting in his eyes.

She glared up at him. "I was wrong about you. You're not any different. Just another asshole cop." She sneered. Jenna spun so fast her ponytail whipped around behind her as she fled the room.

Ribs be damned, Langley dashed after her as she shoved her feet into her boots by the front door.

"Jenna, I'm only trying to—"

"Stop it. Don't try and make—"

But she suddenly ceased talking. Langley heard a muffled buzzing.

"Your phone." Langley said. Jenna's eyes widened. She froze half-way through putting her boot on, her eyes darting between his kitchen and the bedroom door.

Langley raised an eyebrow at her as he saw the whites of her eyes, the sharp inhale of air through her nose.

"Good bye, David." She suddenly announced with finality. Langley managed to open the door for her before she could grab the knob.

Langley did nothing but hold the door open as she finished with her boot, her hands trembling. He was hoping for an admission or explanation, something the detective part of his brain craved to discover about her. He hated the unknowns, the playing of secretive games until someone got emotionally hurt. But acknowledging her issues right now didn't seem to be any better a choice considering her current reaction.

"Jenna," his voice cracked as she looked passed him. She jumped over the threshold of his apartment, pulling out her phone in mid-stride.

He watched the bounce of her ponytail as she shook her head, heard her sniff as she ran to her car.

The Datsun squealed out of the lot and Langley watched the tail lights until another car from the complex pulled out right behind her.

Langley went back inside and slowly shut and locked the door. He sank down on the couch. Then he did something he hadn't done in a decade.

He cried.

CHAPTER TWELVE

HOW THE HELL DID FRANK get my number? Jenna swore as she slammed the Datsun into drive. *And David—that bastard!* She swerved violently onto the main street while blinking away the brightness of the lights from the car behind hers.

Jenna had never been more humiliated in her life; not only had he turned her away sexually, but he had made her into a little pet-project for psychoanalyzing.

Fuck him. She told herself over and over. But the annoying part of her brain kept chiming in. *Except that everything he said was true.*

Jenna pulled into her brother's neighborhood, exceeding the speed limit.

And where would you have been when the phone rang if the asshole cop hadn't stopped you?

She skidded to a stop in front of her brother's house and saw him outside in sweats, waving his own cell phone in the air.

"Jenna!" He roared as she opened the car door. "Where the hell have you been?"

Jenna locked the car quickly and retreated to the garage

where all the neighbors wouldn't hear.

"Answer me!"

"Frank, calm down," Jenna held both hands in front of her.

"Calm down! Are you crazy? I've been looking for you for two hours!"

"Two—why?"

"Because you weren't home!"

"Jesus, Frank, I went to get a drink."

"You didn't tell me."

They were in the garage now; Jenna reached for the door to the house but Frank used a beefy arm to hold it shut. Now pinned, she turned to see that Frank's eyes were wild and bloodshot.

"And why the hell do I need to tell you?" Jenna shot back.

His face and neck darkened under his dusty bandana. "Every stupid thing you do can mess up what I'm doing." He pointed a fat finger inches from her nose. "Did you see that cop again?"

Jenna licked her lips, her head pressed against the door. "No."

Frank dropped his hand but held the ferocity in his tone. "Good. Stay the fuck away from all of them."

"I know, Frank."

"Don't hide shit from me, sis. I know you have a new cell phone, and I got your number." He growled. "Didn't think I was smart enough to figure that out?"

Jenna dropped her chin to her chest, jaw clenched.

Frank coughed a deep, rattling hack before continuing. "You don't go anywhere besides your work without telling me from now on. Or you can get out of my house."

Jenna nodded, hands splayed on the door behind her.

"Jenna," Frank smeared away a wet sniffle with his arm. "I'm trying to protect you."

She brought her gaze up to meet his. "I know, Frank."

"I hope, someday, you really do." He unceremoniously hawked up some phlegm onto the garage floor and turned away from Jenna, boots dragging on the concrete.

Jenna floundered for the knob and stumbled directly to her room.

She wasn't sure what was making her brother so paranoid. But little did he know that after tonight, he'd never have to worry about her meeting with David Langley or any other cop ever again.

Langley was pissed off. Pissed that his evening with Jenna had turned out so badly, pissed at the blue balls caused by thinking about Jenna on a daily basis, pissed at the never-ending pain nagging at his ribs. And now it seemed that everyone in the unit was getting on Langley's last nerve, adding a whole new layer to the pissed-off pie. It had been a hell of a week, and the entire Narcotics Unit gave Langley a wide berth, afraid they might lose an arm if they got to close to the angry Marine.

His unit had screwed up. Two of the detectives had been made in their big case while on watch. It was pathetic. Now the entire team had to switch partners and shifts. The two boneheads that blew it were assigned to the station. Greer and Barnes had been moved and Langley was partnered with an acting detective named Carlson, a young boy that had been making sandwiches before he became a cop and only got assigned to Narcotics because he knew somebody higher up.

The Lieutenant had assigned the pair to perform menial tasks for the day to help update the case and coordinate with the gang task force.

Carlson, however, was killing any productivity Langley was attempting to have. The kid wouldn't shut up, and Langley could not focus on the first sentence of the paper in front of him.

"—so I went over to the house and was like, 'hey guys, check it out, I'm a cop and—"

"Carlson."

"—I've got a badge now and you have to—"

"Carlson."

"Yeah?"

"Shut the fuck up."

"C'mon man, I—"

"Seriously. I cannot do a damned thing with you running your mouth. So please just shut your ass."

"Well, what do you want me to do?"

Langley seized the opportunity and grabbed a thick folder of paperwork.

"Make twenty copies of this, and put each one in a folder for the briefing tomorrow."

The boy slumped, but grabbed the paperwork and headed for the copier.

Langley sank into a chair as he dropped the paper on the desk. He stared at the massive cork board in front of him. There were pictures and snippets of information pinned all over it, identifying every gang member and drug dealer involved in the racket so far. But he wasn't seeing any of it; *You're no different,* she had said. Jenna's words still burned him just as badly as they had that night. He'd spent his entire career thus far trying to prove that he was an honorable police officer, a trustworthy man. *Am I really just another asshole?*

"Lang," Lieutenant Miller yelled as he stepped out of

his office.

"What?"

Miller strode across the room until he stood in front of the board. The Lieutenant rested his fists on Langley's desk, leaning forward.

"What's going on with you?"

"What do you mean?"

"I understand you're still recovering from...everything, but you've been a real dick lately. Anything I should know about?"

Langley frowned. "No, just been a rough month."

"Well, you had better find some joy in life, because Carlson just whined about you to the Captain, and everyone else is avoiding you like the plague. I can't protect you from yourself, and you're walking a fine line right now."

Langley sighed. "I understand."

"I don't want to be forced to make paper on you. You're my best detective and I like you. So put your big boy panties on and let's get back to work with a positive attitude."

"Roger that, Lieutenant."

"Also, I'm glad you haven't shaved." Miller scratched his own jaw in emphasis. "I need you to groom your Dale goatee again. You're going to need it soon."

Miller spun on his heel and marched away. Langley rubbed his hands briskly across his face, then returned to the cork board with a sigh.

Carlson sauntered back in with an armful of folders as Langley finished reorganizing the board.

"Here are the folders."

"Thanks. Set them in the conference room."

Langley grabbed the black jacket hanging on the back of his chair. When Carlson returned, Langley tossed him a set of keys.

"Pull the car around. We'll go check a few leads before the meeting."

Carlson practically ran out of the station with excitement. Langley strolled, barely a hitch in his step now, and straightened his collar as Carlson pulled up. The kid scrambled out of the driver's seat for Langley.

As Langley put it in drive, Carlson, unfortunately, opened his mouth.

"So where are we going?"

"The Saloon."

"What's at The Saloon?"

"A lead."

"What—"

"Carlson."

"I'll shut up."

"Thank you." Langley let the silence hang a moment before speaking again, mostly to stave off Carlson from saying anything else. "How long you been a cop?"

"Two years."

"And what made you want to do narcotics?"

"I think it was not wearing a uniform, being undercover, doing the busts, you know. The good stuff."

Langley suppressed his overwhelming urge to slap him.

"Okay. Were you assigned temporarily?"

"Yeah."

"Pending what, exactly?" Langley turned the steering wheel, glancing at all his mirrors.

"Captain Worly said until this case was over. He said the department needed all available hands in Narcotics with the FBI coming over. Oh, I mean—"

"So the Feds are in on this?"

"I don't know."

Langley braked hard and skidded to a stop at the red

light, tires squealing. He turned and leaned over into Carlson's face; Carlson's head hit the passenger window with a dull thud as he made an attempt to avoid smacking noses with Langley. They were inches apart; Langley could smell the donuts and coffee on the rookie's breath as his injured torso strained from the sudden torque.

"You're lying. Don't lie to me, Carlson. Spill it."

"Well, that's what he said. The Feds, maybe DEA. Especially since the two detectives got made, it makes the department look bad and now the FBI wants to take over. Captain said he'd be willing to work with them if they prosecute federally. That and they have to share all their info with us. Uh, the light's green."

Langley returned to his side of the car and started driving again as Carlson sank back into his seat.

"Like that will ever happen," Langley mumbled, looking over his left shoulder at a motorcycle that was roaring past their car. A pang of longing hit him as he watched it speed by; he missed his bike, which was currently stashed away for his undercover persona.

"What, the FBI stepping in?"

"No, them sharing information."

"Aren't we all on the same side, you know, against the gangs?"

Langley snorted as he flashed his turn signal to change lanes. "Every agency has an agenda, Carlson. Would you show everyone at the poker table your cards with the hopes that they will show you theirs?"

"No. I mean, right?"

Langley pulled into a parking spot at the back of the closed bar.

"No, you wouldn't. Because in the end, only one person can win, and everyone else gets diddly, and some jackass always cheats and has an ace up his sleeve. The FBI is stepping in because we can't handle the task, but there's always a bigger picture. Don't forget that."

"Okay."

"Now let's go do our job. But Carlson, let me do the talking."

Jenna couldn't decide whether she wanted to scream or cry. Decidedly, she buried her head into her pillow and screamed. Moments later, she dropped the pillow and let out a long sigh, staring at her cell phone sitting on the floor.

No new job opportunities for her, and the asshole David Langley's words kept bouncing around in her brain like a bad TV jingle, annoying the hell out of her at the most inopportune times. *You're not telling me something...don't want you to do anything you're not mentally prepared for.*

Jenna could vehemently deny it to everyone, but deep down she knew that David had seen more than just a glimpse of hesitation. *You were right, cop. And now I'll tell you nothing.*

She had never been so mortified in her life; to be turned down and rejected when he'd been the one giving off all the signs that inevitably should have led to some mind-blowing sex. Jenna still got heated when thinking about it; and yet, her rational brain kept obnoxiously knocking. *He knows you're an emotional wreck,* it mocked her. *And he wants the truth more than he wants the sex.*

That sudden realization hit her hard. Her anger was briefly surpassed by a sense of serenity. She took a moment to truly ponder his actions that night; *he saved you, Jenna. From both your own shame and any chance of regret. You can't deny it.*

Jenna inhaled deeply, feeling lightheaded. She had

definitely lied to him that night. David Langley was completely different than any man she'd ever met, and now she had to deal with the guilt of belittling him on her way out his door. *What kind of man turns down sex just to talk about my traumas?* Jenna wondered if she'd ever get the chance to tell him she now understood why he'd pushed her away—or the chance to tell him anything at all.

Forget it. He's long gone now.

Jenna cleared her throat, wiping her hands down her shirt as if brushing David Langley from her life. But, try as she might, she couldn't forget the way his solid jaw had felt in her hands, the way he moaned against her lips as they kissed. Jenna growled aloud as she clenched her fists at her sides.

I wonder if he's already forgotten me.

CHAPTER THIRTEEN

"Thanks for all your help, Mrs. Pierce."

"Of course. I'll let you boys know if I see anything else."

They shook hands. Carlson and Langley exited the bar, Langley tucking his small notepad back into his pants pocket.

"So that was good, right?"

"It was helpful."

"I mean, now we've got descriptions and times—"

"Can you wait until we get to the car?"

"Right. Sorry."

Langley sighed as he unlocked the doors and slid into the driver's seat. *This kid should never work undercover, he's going to get someone killed.*

As he started driving, Langley could tell the kid was dying to open his mouth to say something. He enjoyed the moments of peace, knowing they wouldn't last.

"So..."

Langley turned the clamor of the police radio up a bit and listened to Woods go back and forth with dispatch. It was soothing in comparison to Carlson.

However, speech was inevitable and Langley spoke before Carlson could ask another question.

"Yes, Carlson. We have some good insight as to who is involved with the real drug deals and who might be supplying. But nothing is concrete, and some of the other under-covers are trying to set up a sting to net the lot of them."

"Yeah, okay."

"Now we're going to scope out a few of the better known hang-outs, then we're going back to the station."

"Cool."

Langley was surprised that the kid stayed quiet for most of the drive. There was nothing out of the ordinary, no new cars or bikes at the hot spots. Langley parked the car and handed Carlson the keys as they entered the station.

As Langley stooped over his desk, he heard the muffled shouts of his Lieutenant behind closed doors. He could not make out words, only a good deal of high decibel, one-sided conversation.

Hoping it was not going to roll from Miller to him, Langley decided to ignore it and focus on his last task of the evening. He rubbed his sore ribs, grateful he could finally take almost a full breath, and started typing the notes from his meeting with Mrs. Pierce.

Carlson was drumming a pen at Greer's desk; with one fierce look from Langley he dropped the pen and put his hands up in surrender. In the background, Langley heard a phone slam onto a receiver.

"Carlson, look busy and unimportant when LT opens that door."

"What do you—" but his words were cut short as the Lieutenant emitted a string of profanity from his now open doorway. Carlson dove into a pile of paperwork, scanning it as if he were deep in thought.

"Who's here!" Miller barked, breezing through the row of desks. "Langley!"

"Yessir?" Langley responded, immediately locking eyes with his superior.

"We're really in the shit. That was some FBI special sucker on the line, says our operation now has to 'mesh' with theirs. Chief even talked to me and tried to demand I relinquish all our records."

Langley saw Carlson gulp, his eyes darting from him to the back of Miller's head. *This kid is a blow it.*

"What can I do to help, boss?"

"They are all coming to the briefing. Tomorrow."

It took another two hours to prep the office, set up the conference room, relocate and put the final touches on the boards and finalize the briefing. Miller was a wreck, knowing this case could make or break his career as well as Brookside Police Department's entire reputation. They already had two people on the team screw up part of the operation and Langley did not want any more attention drawn to him, the department, or anyone else.

When everything was prepped, the three men left the station in silence, an odd group of policemen. Langley could only wonder how the FBI was going to handle working with the lot of them.

It could be worse, Langley thought to himself. There were six of them in total, all of them Feds. Langley couldn't remember their names and didn't care to. The briefing was awkward and forced, but they got through it. Now it was the hashing of the boundaries, trying to figure out who was going to work where and how they were going to do this now that there were twice as many kids on the playground.

The FBI suit in charge of the whole operation was an absolute asshole. Langley knew Miller was going to have problems keeping any sort of rein on the guy, and Langley hoped he wouldn't directly cross paths with him. He was a short, demeaning, beady-eyed and pursed-lipped prick.

Langley did his best wallflower impression as the discussion grew deeper. The prick—Agent Keene—was demanding complete control of the inevitable sting operation, but Miller coerced Keene into organizing a joint task force where Brookside detectives could float under either jurisdiction.

And of course, the FBI agents would now be doing most of the surveillance. That was no surprise. He heard Carlson's name come up; Carlson was assigned to the role of administrative help. Greer was hitting the streets undercover again to work out the final deal, Barnes was pushing reports, Neil was going undercover as well to see if he could do some infiltrating at the lower level. More of Langley's unit was assigned to phone taps and computer monitoring. Brookside's Gang Task Force was in full support, doing what they normally do. When it finally got to Langley, all six FBI agents looked at him as if he were tonight's meal.

"Didn't you get run over or something?"

Langley stared blankly at Keene, not giving him the satisfaction of a response.

"Are you fit for duty?"

"Sure am." Langley's voice reverberated around the conference room.

"We'll see," Keene sniffed. "You're with me and Harris for now, that way your department has someone to report back for them."

"Roger that." Langley covered his distaste with feigned

arrogance, pretending that sucking up to the Feds was all he'd ever dreamed of. Langley saw the stocky man named Harris roll his eyes after sharing a glance with Keene.

Great. Langley put on his game face as the meeting came to a close. *As if life couldn't possibly get any worse, now I'm the FBI's interim secretary.*

Langley felt useless. Keene and Harris were tight-lipped and hardly ever spoke in front of Langley. Their days were spent staring at the office boards, driving around and listening to day-old audio recordings of drunken men talking about porn, beer and smoking weed. Langley thought he might lose his mind. He was getting an uneasy feeling that something was amiss; the rising tension in the office was palatable and it felt as if the investigation was at a stand-still.

Langley had also been deeply hoping that Jenna might call him after figuring out that he was looking out after her best interests that night, but that hadn't happened either. *Looks like I was the fool after all,* Langley mused. He couldn't shake the image of her trembling and crying, or how badly he still wanted to wrap his arms around her, protect her from whatever was causing her so much emotional turmoil. *Get over it. She hates you, remember? You're nothing but an asshole cop.*

Langley blinked rapidly as he shook his head. He was not reading the analysis in front of him even though he'd been trying for twenty minutes.

Carlson was busy listening to some recording through a set of headphones when Keene suddenly flew out of the conference room at a full gallop, arms flailing and suit coat flapping.

Keene dove into Carlson's desk, ripped the headphones out of the computer and choked Carlson with the cord trying to get the earphones off of his head. Carlson yowled as Langley rose from his desk and covered the ground between them in seconds.

Fists raised, Langley was cocked back to deal a knock-out blow to Keene's asshole mouth when Miller came screaming into the room at a sprint.

"What in the hell—"

"You are not authorized to any of this!" Keene bellowed, wielding the headphones like a shield against Langley. "This is part of FBI investigation only, not privy to the department." Miller pushed Langley aside to get in Keene's face.

"And why the hell not?" Miller matched Keene's decibel level. "Last time I checked, we were monitoring airwaves before you got here!"

"Not anymore. Relinquish, or I swear I'll completely obliterate you and your half-ass operation." Keene threw the headphones at Miller's chest. "Your incompetency can be tolerated in the field, but not with something as sensitive as this."

Miller had caught the headphones and immediately threw them back at Carlson. Langley stood behind his Lieutenant, trying to figure out what was causing this sudden showdown. Keene sneered at Miller; Langley's boss ultimately chose the high road.

"Fine. Carlson, move this equipment wherever that...Agent wants it."

"It's going out into my van. All of it."

"Suit yourself," Miller snapped. "Though I deserve an explanation."

Keene glowered. "You deserve nothing until this investigation is closed. Once that happens, you can have whatever you want."

Miller blinked. Langley realized that his Lieutenant no longer held any power over anything involving the operation. Keene's priggish smirk denoted he had come to the same conclusion.

Keene waved his hand at Harris. Carlson scrambled out of the way as Harris grabbed the equipment and headed out the door.

Miller let loose a string of profanity as he vigorously scratched his neck. They all stood there awkwardly as Keene stormed back to the conference room. Langley frowned at Miller, but they remained silent as Harris returned. Harris ducked under Keene's arm to get inside the conference room before Keene slammed the door, neither of them glancing back.

Langley turned to his Lieutenant who was turning a shade of purple. "What in the hell is going on?"

Miller turned to regard Langley. "I don't know. If you figure it out, fill me in." Miller spun on his heels and retreated to his office.

Carlson and Langley were left in a daze.

"Langley," Carlson suddenly whispered. The kid looked like an owl as he swung his head in both directions, whites of his eyes showing.

"What?"

Carlson put a finger to his lips in a silent shush and beckoned Langley closer. Glancing at the conference room, Langley took a knee in front of Carlson's desk and Carlson leaned all the way down between the computer monitors to whisper to Langley.

"They're monitoring *us*."

"What? Why?"

"I don't know. But nothing on their waves right now was about drugs, it was all our desk phones and Miller's conversations."

"We already monitor ourselves, and they are sitting right here next to us all day. That's ridiculous."

Carlson seemed frantic as he hoarsely croaked. "I'm telling the truth!"

"I know. I'm just confused." Langley put his hands on the desk, but before he stood he leaned closer. "Carlson. Trust me. You didn't hear anything, alright? Don't tell anyone about this."

"Okay Langley. I won't, I promise."

Langley stood and slowly turned to walk back to his desk.

"Hey, Detective." It was Keene, still holding the knob to the conference room door.

"Yes?" Langley put a hand casually on his sidearm, shifted the holster back.

Keene flicked his head upward and toward the conference room. Langley dropped his arms and strolled over; Keene shut the door behind him as Harris sat on the conference table.

As if nothing had just happened, Keene dove right into work, acting as if Langley hadn't just been about to smash a fist into his face.

"Who's usually in for face-to-face time with Danny?" Keene pointed to a picture of one of their informants, a runner for the main drug dealer, a man called 'Red.'

"Greer and myself, sometimes Barnes." Langley realized they were looking for a deeper explanation when Keene kept staring. "Greer heads it, he's the main under cover. I'm his 'cousin'. I run some small deals for authenticity and general reconnaissance. Barnes will sometimes go in and chat up the ladies to see what she can find out and she goes as my girlfriend."

"Why haven't you all remained under for the duration of this op?"

Langley shrugged dejectedly. He'd asked Miller the same thing at the start of it all a few months ago, knowing full well that they were putting themselves at huge risk by playing both sides of the aisle so casually.

"Lack of funds, lack of detectives and a serious lack of operational security."

Harris snorted. "Well, I'll be damned. At least you're honest about that." Harris threw his hands up in the air as he leaned back on the table. "How haven't you three been made?"

Langley wasn't trying to betray his department, but he had no answer and he was not one to lie. "Luck."

"Let's hope you stay lucky. Starting now, we need you in until we're done. You've got a party to go to. Harris and I can't go because we're not invited and there's not enough time to introduce us. But thanks to Danny, you three are in." Keene slid a paper in front of Langley. "Red's daughter's twenty-first birthday, and he's having quite a bash."

Langley nodded slowly. "When?"

"Saturday."

"Are you handling us, or is Miller?" Langley questioned as he sat down on the edge of the conference table next to Harris, casually swinging a leg back and forth.

Harris grunted as Keene answered. "Us. But Miller will be alongside, don't worry."

"I'm not." As Langley looked over the report, he felt both their gazes lingering far too long. "Should I be worried?"

Keene pursed his lips together as his eyebrows shot up. "You tell me."

Langley blinked. Langley wasn't certain what Keene

was implying; he did his best to keep his confusion placated. "I'm sure I'll get the details tomorrow?"

Keene nodded. "See you in the morning, Dale Clark."

Langley gave a small nod as he rose from the table, a knot in his gut.

Here we go.

CHAPTER FOURTEEN

LANGLEY SHIFTED INTO HIS role fully during the next week. He revved his motorcycle for the first time in two months; it had been squirreled away in storage at the back of his buddy's house waiting for his return to undercover work. He charged the cruddy cell phone used by his alter-ego Dale. He fully embraced band shirts, worn jeans and refrained from showering. He started hanging back out at the Saloon in the evenings, joking and laughing with the lower-level informants and dealers he'd already built a rapport with.

Greer ("Gary," now) had already been back to his undercover work with a much more sophisticated cover. He was a better schmoozer and was buttering up the bigger fish while Langley dealt with identifying the users and lowers. Greer played the part of a high-fluting college administrator with a hankering for moving meth and heroine. Barnes ("Bailey") was looking hot in her leather boots and bandannas, flirting with some new faces while sipping a beer. It seemed surreal to be thrust back into this world after all Langley had been through in the past few months.

The board at the office was getting a daily face lift, and

Agent Keene seemed to be legitimately enjoying himself while running the three of them. Carlson and Harris managed the Detectives' wireless wires as a duo, transmitting audio directly back to the office for monitoring.

Saturday approached quickly. Langley was dressed at his worst and had stayed up most of the night before in an effort to look authentically strung out. He spent the afternoon working on his bike, getting his hands greasy and not making much effort to wash it off. He polished a spot on his old low rider before hitting the street.

He picked Barnes up at the cover house and drove to the evening party, parking his bike in line with another thirty bikes outside an amazingly maintained mansion.

There was music, beer, shots and dancers. Correction: male dancers. Langley sauntered through the crowd effortlessly, meshing well with everyone he crossed paths with while scratching at his goatee. He had already found some new dealers and was expanding the dragnet when Danny finally tracked him down.

"Dale, bro!" Danny called out. Langley embraced the informant and they clanked their beer bottles together. "I've got someone for you to meet, man. I think you'll like him, he's as big as a house."

The phrase made no logical sense, but to Langley and everyone back at the office listening to the live-streaming audio through Langley, it meant the target operated one of the stash houses.

Langley allowed himself to be led from the massive living-room-gone-dance-floor to the backyard which was lit with tiki lamps and neon pool lights. Palm trees lined the wall and benches surrounded the faux rock pool.

To the normal eye, it looked like any other house party. All walks of life were meandering around enjoying themselves. Langley was analyzing and processing more than just the festivities; he'd already marked two new low-time dealers and had purchased some meth, which was sitting in his pocket. The small audio-transmitting pen cap was tucked inside his ragged, 1972 denim jacket purchased at the thrift store years prior and his boots scuffed along the concrete as he dragged his feet.

"You looking thin, man." Danny said to him as they made their way around the pool, dancing with some scantily clad ladies as they passed.

Langley responded by smiling at him crookedly, his red-tinged goatee splitting to reveal white teeth. *If you only knew.*

"Dale, I want you to meet Peppermint Patty. Call 'im P-Pat."

Now, this was someone new indeed. Langley had never even heard of this fellow. Langley extended a hand, but received none in return. The man was eye level with Langley at six feet and his blue eyes were cool, calm. His bandana was supposed to be red, and his boots were supposed to be black. Instead, both were the color of dust.

"There's got to be a hell of a story behind the name," Langley offered, swaggering to the side of the man called P-Pat so they were both looking back toward the house, standing shoulder to shoulder. *These guys have such stupid nicknames.*

The man still didn't speak. Langley couldn't decipher whether he was nervous or just plain irritated by Langley's presence. His chubby arms were crossed over his broad chest, a beer bottle in one hand. He was glaring across the pool.

"Danny tells me you're a family friend." He finally offered with a deep, raspy voice, followed by the hocking of an ungodly loogie into the palm trees behind him. Langley did his best to hide how grossed out he was by wiping a hand across his own nose.

"I worked on his mom's beamer, gave him a great deal on a drive shaft repair. Also fixed his shitty ride. Hey, if you ever need any work done, tell Danny and I'll be there for you, man." Langley gave his shoulder a quick pat and flashed a smile.

"I'll keep it in mind." He glanced at Langley's grease-stained hand and blew off Langley's ramble, as intended.

Langley had been studying the outside crowd and finally spotted Red, the head of the drug ring. He was kissing his daughter on the cheek and adorned her with a birthday crown. The girl was radiant in a sparkling red dress that hugged her shapely young body. Langley saw P-Pat's eyes lingering on her.

Barnes had sauntered over at that point and Langley gave her a smooch on the cheek.

"P, this is my girlfriend Bailey."

The man called P-Pat showed a bit more respect for her introduction and actually took her outstretched hand and gave it a peck. Barnes feigned her greatest pleasure as Langley played grab-ass, until he heard a voice. A voice that plagued his mind every day with its insults and tore at his heartstrings.

"Hey bro, have you seen Lenny? He left his phone in my car."

Oh shit.

Jenna had only agreed to go to the party because Frank had promised her that someone he knew that worked for the ambulance company would be there. She had been waiting for the guy for an hour without luck, and Frank had been standing at the back of the pool glowering the entire time.

She'd given some of his outrageously smelly buddies a ride in her car, but one of the idiots had left his phone on her seat and she'd spotted it, so she'd been carrying it around ever since looking for its owner.

Although the party was lavish, she didn't really care about anyone there. Not even the male dancers were striking her fancy. None of them seemed to compare to the thought of the chivalrous David Langley, even though they sported seriously chiseled abs and biceps the size of cantaloupes.

Flustered, Jenna was making her way around the crowds looking for the biker named Lenny. Finally giving up, she decided to ask Frank even though he'd told her to steer clear of him during the party.

As she made her way towards her brother, she saw a couple nearby biting each others' ears and groping one another. *Jesus, get a room already.* She huffed.

"Hey bro, have you seen Lenny? He left his phone in my car."

And then the sleazy pair turned to regard her, and Jenna met the steady gaze of the greasy man beside her brother.

Jenna froze, her mouth half open.

The red goatee and the general filthiness was not enough to conceal the fierce copper eyes that she'd been seeing in her mind every day, the haunted look that she'd never forget as those eyes stared up at her from the asphalt.

Almost imperceptibly, a grungy David Langley shook his head once, slowly, back and forth, his jaw clamped shut and his lips thin.

Jenna's brain went complete scramble. A hundred different thoughts and questions all collided into her mind at once, rendering her completely immobile. Jenna wasn't sure how much time had passed before she heard distant voices.

"Hello?" Frank was saying. "What the fuck's wrong with you?"

"I...uh, what?"

"You okay, honey?" asked the woman clinging to Langley.

Jenna blinked. *Is she a cop, too? Oh Jesus.*

"Sure someone didn't slip something into your drink?" Langley said, his voice slightly slurred and higher pitched. He let go of the woman's ass and took a step toward her. Jenna expected Frank to say something, but instead her brother glared silently at the back of Langley's head.

"No, I'm not sure." Jenna groaned.

And then Langley was there, standing before her, his powerful arms cloaked by a worn out jacket, but still so wonderfully warm. He took her arm in his and walked her casually to a bench as if he were a walking an old lady across a busy street.

"You ought to be more careful." Langley cleared his throat. Her brother was watching them closely as Langley sat Jenna down on a bench at the back of the yard, about ten paces away from Frank.

"I'm Dale, by the way." Langley had seen Jenna was about to speak and quickly cut her off. "And you are a bit screwed up at the moment."

"Yes. Yes I am." Jenna was starting to get her wits back, but as a result she was shaking uncontrollably. *Langley—undercover—Oh my God, what am I in the middle of?*

"Breathe." For that moment, he was the David Langley she knew, his deep voice resonating within her. It only addled her more.

"What—"

Langley hunched his shoulders as he coughed loudly, his index finger pointing to his chest.

Of course. He's wired.

His lips moved soundlessly. *Not now,* he mouthed, the whites of his bloodshot eyes revealing genuine panic. He reached down and grabbed her hands in his, his bulky jacket blocking the view of the party goers.

Jenna realized in that moment that he was terrified as well—terrified that she was going to blow his cover either intentionally or unintentionally, and who knows what the consequences were for that.

"Thank you, Dale." Jenna swallowed as she regarded the intensity in his fierce glare. "I'll be fine."

Langley squeezed her hands. She couldn't tell if it was her hands that were trembling, or his.

CHAPTER FIFTEEN

LANGLEY WAS UNPREPARED for such an emotional roller coaster, and it took him a few moments to compose himself after Jenna finally started coming around. Langley glanced back and saw Barnes carrying a water bottle, heading their way.

"Here," Langley took the bottle from Barnes and placed it in Jenna's hand. Barnes sidled up beside Langley, looking hard at Jenna.

"You doing better?"

"Yes, thank you. I'll be fine." Jenna cracked the bottle open and took a long drink.

"Alright honey. Take it easy." Barnes slipped her arm into Langley's elbow. Langley put a hand around Barnes' waist, but his eyes lingered on Jenna.

Langley was thankful she hadn't completely blown it, but the party was still just getting started. *Gee, I wonder if this has anything to do with what she doesn't want to tell you?* Langley internally glowered. The similarities between P-Pat and her were obvious to him now; the misty blue eyes, the blonde-tinged sandy hair. She had called him 'bro'. *The stash house's sister. Great.*

Barnes was leading Langley away from Jenna, who was still shaking on the bench. Langley felt hollow as he turned away.

"I swear she looks familiar," Barnes whispered into Langley's ear.

He grunted, not offering to make the connection to Woods' dash cam video. Langley couldn't control the perspiration running down his spine, or the slight tremor in his hand. At least his ailments only added to his authenticity as a druggie, but Langley was still having a difficult time focusing on anything.

"Dude, are you okay?" Barnes was still holding his arm and they were back inside the house on a corner of the dance floor. She'd leaned into his neck to ask the question so no one else would hear.

Langley's sigh was little more than a rattling breath as he mopped his forehead with the sleeve of his jacket. "I'm good."

She nodded, studying his face with eyes that sparkled from the disco balls hanging above them.

Pull yourself together, man. You've a job to do.

They watched Greer make his rounds in a suit, swirling a glass of wine idly with one hand.

Jenna seemed to have disappeared, which was good for Langley's psyche. He forced himself back into the game and started making his way toward P-Pat and a few other bikers that had gathered around the pool, all staring towards the birthday girl dancing with the strippers.

Langley saw a few of their hands dip into pockets and waistbands, doing the normal nervous-check on weapons and drugs.

"You Gary's cousin?" One of them asked as he approached.

"That's me. Dale," he stuck out a hand and the man shook it briskly.

"Rick."

Langley scratched his neck and eyed P-Pat. *Jenna's brother*, he reminded himself. One of the new dealers he'd pegged was also standing there, peddling something to another biker.

"Heard you do decent work on bikes." Rick put a hand into his pocket and watched Langley coolly. "Can you fix the rattling in my Cross Bones?"

Langley nodded with a sniff. "Sure. When?"

Rick chuckled. "You that bent, man?"

Langley forced a fake jittery smile as he twiddled his fingers around his still-full beer. "Sure as shit, always looking for a fix, bro. Start it up, I'll tell you what's wrong."

Rick gestured with a thick hand towards the house. Langley led the way to the front, bumping into Red on the way out. They exchanged mumbled apologies as Rick walked the line of bikes in the huge circle driveway.

Motorcycles were everywhere and men were revving bikes, drinking beers and cursing about their bikes. Women were stroking handlebars and clinging to old fat men and young buff boys alike. The smell of marijuana was everywhere.

Rick plopped himself down onto the seat of his Cross Bones and started it. He took a ride around the driveway during a lull in the symphony of Harleys.

Langley listened and caught a glimpse of Jenna out of the corner of his eye. She was half-engaged in a conversation with some guy Langley hadn't met, her arms clinging to her own shoulders in the crisp night air.

When Rick cut the engine, Langley put his palms up. "Seriously, bro? All you need to do is tighten your baffles.

Tape the shit or I'll come by and saw 'em off for you."

Rick nodded, his chin jutted out. "You got a card?"

Langley laughed. "Nah man. I work off word of mouth. Take down my number." Rick entered Langley's cover cell number into his phone. *This asshole had better go down with the rest of them when this is over.*

Langley ignored Jenna as he walked back inside. He spotted Barnes flirting with P-Pat, and he was smiling and laughing with her. Not a good time to interrupt as she seemed to be getting a lot done, so Langley opted to sit at an empty stool and watch the girls on the dance floor while he faked drinking a beer.

Some nasty woman sat next to him for a bit, ogling his jeans and looking for a hit of something, crack or weed. Langley shooed her away and secretly prayed that Greer and Barnes were wrapping things up.

He's already scored enough evidence and had identified a few more people that would get arrested during the multi-agency sweep, whenever that might occur. Greer was in charge of setting that exact operation up right now, and he seemed to be actively engaged with Red in the kitchen.

Good. I need to get some sleep. Langley rubbed his eyes and when he opened them, Barnes was in front of him, a knee on his bar stool between his legs.

"Get me the hell out of here," she whispered as she faked licking his ear. "Some guy just tried to slip me ecstasy."

"My pleasure," Langley said loudly, grabbing her neck. "Just let me piss first."

She sauntered towards the front door, licking her lips as she passed all the patrons listening in on their conversation.

Langley really did have to piss. He made his way to a

restroom, made sure the drugs were still in his pocket as he handled his business, then opened the bathroom door, ready to get home and sleep this one off.

Jenna was standing right outside the door, whites of her eyes glowing in the dim lighting.

Langley put a finger to his lips immediately, glancing back towards the party.

She put her fists to her mouth and bit her knuckle, like a scared child who'd just had a nightmare. A single tear trickled down her cheek as she sniffed.

Langley barely had time to spare another look down the hallway before Jenna threw herself into his arms; Langley wrapped his arms around her and slipped a hand through the back of her soft hair, pulling her flush against him so that her head rested on his chest. He kissed the top of her head as he tightly embraced her. Jenna's trembling hands found his chest and she clutched his shirt for a moment before looking up into Langley's eyes.

In that moment, Langley wanted nothing more than to protect her; he felt the surge of adrenaline, the rush of the fierce defensive instinct that had been instilled in him for a decade. His muscles flexed and his jaw clenched as he glared down the hallway, holding her in his arms.

Langley returned to her glimmering blue eyes. He quickly lowered his head and brushed his lips against hers, tasting the salt of her tears. But Langley knew the four seconds it had taken to give Jenna that small comfort was risky enough, so he smoothly detached her hands and headed straight down the hallway without looking back.

Barnes was waiting on the back of his bike and there was no hesitation as he kicked off the asphalt and roared the bike down the driveway.

Keene and Miller were waiting inside Barnes' cover

house for Langley and Barnes. Once out of the public eye, the pair did drug tests, processed their evidence, turned over their wires and did a lengthy debrief.

"You look like hell, Lang." Miller glared at Langley.

"Thank you." Langley flashed a smile he didn't feel. "I've been up for more than thirty hours, my ribs hurt and I smell like greasy ass."

Miller seemed distraught, but he ended up just shaking his head. "Okay Langley. Get some sleep. Good work." He clapped Langley on the shoulder, lingered a little longer than Langley expected.

Frowning, Langley headed for the door after giving Barnes a fist bump. Keene hadn't said a word, which struck Langley as odd. *I'm too tired to care.*

Langley practically dragged himself to the door of his apartment after checking his surroundings numerous times. No one was out, and no one had followed him. He'd walked his bike almost a block to keep the noise down.

He unlocked his door and slipped inside; when he went to pull the door closed behind him, he felt the door abruptly jolt backwards and saw a shadowy form clutching at the knob. Expecting an ambush, Langley drew his pistol instantly and placed his finger in the trigger guard.

CHAPTER SIXTEEN

JENNA HAD BEEN HIDING in the stupid bushes for almost an hour waiting for David Langley. Her initial fear which she'd felt at the party was slowly being replaced by anger—anger at not knowing what David was doing, frustrated at the secrets he was keeping from her. When he finally staggered into view, Jenna couldn't stop the fear and rage from taking over her common sense.

When he'd unlocked the door and slid quickly inside his apartment, she hastily grabbed his door knob and yanked the door open; Langley spun violently and had his concealed revolver drawn and leveled in less than a second.

"Whoa!" Jenna exhaled in a rush, immediately opening and lifting her hands to her chest as she took a step backward.

His eyes were wild and the muscles in his jaw flexed as he emitted a throaty growl; the handgun immediately lowered when realization set in, but the hostility in his glare remained. He quickly grabbed Jenna and pulled her inside, peeking his head out the door before closing it silently and locking it. He holstered his weapon with a trembling hand, his jaw rigid as he narrowed his eyes at Jenna.

"Don't ever sneak up on me like that again." Langley snarled. He took a shaky breath and glanced at the ground before his eyes fiercely regarded Jenna once more. "What are you even doing here?" He growled. Jenna was standing in the living room as he ran his grease-stained hands through his disheveled hair. "Are you trying to get me killed?"

"I deserve an expla—"

Langley suddenly grabbed her shoulders hard, his thumbs digging into her chest muscles. "Did anyone follow you here?" His bloodshot eyes were panicked.

"Why would anyone follow—"

Langley groaned as he released her, putting his palms to his eyes.

"Why have you been following me!" Jenna shouted. Langley shushed her as she continued. "Since the bar you've been, what, investigating me?"

Langley tore off his jacket in one swift motion and threw it on the couch.

"Don't flatter yourself." He sneered, scratching his goatee. He starting groping at his boots next, discarding them by the door as she continued.

"What were you doing at that party? And why are you—"

"Stop!" Langley hissed, clapping his hand over her mouth as he closed the gap between them instantly, his eyes wild. "Dammit!" He grunted through gritted teeth. "I'm not investigating *you*. I am trying to do my job, which involves this type of work. It's not hard to figure out why *I* was at that kind of a party." He pushed her lightly away from him, enough to get her to take a step back. "The real question is, why were *you* at that party?"

Jenna flared her nostrils. "My brother introduced me to a manager at AMR in the hopes of getting my foot in for a job."

Langley's gaze did not move from her face as he tore his socks off and tossed them on the couch with the jacket. "Fascinating." He said lightly, raising his shoulders in a prolonged shrug. "And, please, why don't you tell me a little about your brother?" Langley started tugging at his belt buckle.

Jenna's mouth went dry. *Of course he's not following me. Jenna, you idiot!*

"You—you're using me to get to my *brother*?"

Jenna watched sweat trickle down Langley's neck. He was breathing in short breaths, his hands shaking as he fought with the belt still stuck in his pant loops. "No. I didn't know your brother existed until today." He stopped pulling on his belt to glare at Jenna with narrowed copper eyes. "Which means you are either working me for him, or you are an ignorant fool."

Jenna snarled. "How *dare* you—"

"I have an idea." Langley interrupted, yanking the rest of his belt out in one hard tug. He grimaced and grabbed his side, talking through gritted teeth. "Why don't we start this entire conversation over." Langley grabbed the bottom of his shirt with one hand and hastily stripped it off as he stormed towards the bedroom. Jenna balked as he continued his shucking of clothing, trying not to let her gaze linger on his muscled back while Langley seemed oblivious and engrossed in his own world. He stopped in the doorway, one arm holding the frame as a tense silence fell between them. Langley shook his head slowly with a loud sigh. "Look, I'm not trying to upset you, Jenna. But I need the truth. You're hiding so many secrets that I can't even begin to guess what's going on, or what your true purpose is in coming here to my place tonight."

Langley turned in the doorway, wearing nothing but a filthy pair of jeans, sweat beading on his chiseled chest and abs. Jenna was woozy, both from the conversation and his lack of clothing.

"Jenna," Langley leaned on his door frame and massaged his muscled shoulder, his tone suddenly mellow. He looked down at the ground before bringing his gaze up to meet hers. "Something is haunting you, I can see it in your eyes. I realize that asking for the truth is making you choose sides and will open those old wounds. I'm not asking you to betray your brother." He took one step towards her. "But you should know that he's betraying *you*. I want the truth, but what I want more than anything in this world is to keep you safe, and if that means protecting you from your own brother, I will do it without hesitation."

Jenna held her breath, her knees quivering as Langley held both his hands out and took another step, emitting a deep sigh before continuing. "But I can't protect you from any of this if I don't know what's going on." He was close enough now for Jenna to feel the radiating heat of his body; she looked down to the place where his abs disappeared beneath his jeans. Sucking in a breath through her nose, she tried to concentrate on what he was saying. Jenna blinked rapidly as his hot palm caressed her shoulder gently before lifting her chin and forcing her gaze to meet his. "So, before I put my entire career and life on the line for you, I need to know. Are you with me, or are you with them?"

Langley felt queasy as he preyed on Jenna's emotions. He hadn't wanted it to come to this, but she was dangerously close to blowing everything and both of them would end up in hot water if he didn't get to the bottom of this mess right now.

Jenna caved. She collapsed into him, her hands splayed on his slippery chest as she emitted a quiet cry. Langley embraced her and relished the surge of heat that ran through him as Jenna's body pressed against his; he waited minutes before gently grasping her shoulders.

"Jenna," Langley whispered as he brought his nose an inch from hers, their gazes fixated. "Take some time, sit down and think about this." Langley dragged his fingers down her arm until he reached her hand. He gently pulled her towards the bedroom and she did not resist. "I desperately need a shower. If you're still here when I get out, we'll talk through everything together. You need some time alone to think." She sank down on the side of Langley's bed with her gaze focused on the floor.

Langley knelt down in front of her as she remained silent. He was eye level with her chest, but she was now forced to look at him instead of the ground. "If you decide to leave, then this is goodbye and whatever happens is out of my control. The decision is yours. Just know that I must do my job regardless." Langley watched a tear roll down her flushed cheeks. He reached to wipe it away and hesitated, but Jenna did not recoil. Langley brushed his finger across her soft cheek.

He stood and turned without looking back, closing the restroom door behind him.

You've got her, the investigative part of his brain rejoiced. But he felt an impending sense of dread even though he knew he would never willingly betray her trust.

Langley slipped out of his pants and boxers and stepped into the shower, savoring the blast of cold water before it turned hot. He scrubbed himself over twice and was thinking through what might transpire after his shower when he heard the shower door abruptly slide open.

Langley froze, hot water cascading over his shoulders as a completely nude Jenna stepped in, her eyes puffy and her hair loose. She closed the door behind her, her blue eyes focused on nothing but his face. Her chin lifted just a fraction as she breathed in deeply before speaking.

"I'm with you."

CHAPTER SEVENTEEN

LANGLEY BLINKED. Jenna stood rigid before him, almost at attention, as water began to splatter on her eyelashes. It ran down her slender neck and over her breasts, sliding down her flat abdomen. Langley was riveted in place, absorbing the beauty of her sensual curves, the way her chest slowly rose with each breath.

Their slick bodies collided as one; Jenna wrapped her arms around his neck and Langley encircled her back as their lips crushed together. Langley ran a hand down her spine and she arched into him, her skin slick against his chest; she moaned against his mouth and Langley shivered as her tongue teased his lip. The hot water streamed down their faces and washed the salt of Jenna's tears away.

Langley bent to cup her ass, his hands lifting her slightly off the ground as he deepened the kiss, relishing the heat of her tongue against his. She pressed her body hard against his while clutching his broad shoulders. Jenna reached up to run her hands through his short hair, then scraped her nails down the back of his neck. Langley shuddered at her touch; he slowly relaxed his hands and brought them up to her firm waist, feeling her hips flex beneath his hands.

She dragged her nails down his back, sending a shock of pleasure through Langley that made him gasp aloud, breaking their kiss.

Langley slammed the shower off and Jenna flung open the door. Jenna grabbed the towel hanging on the wall and wrapped herself in it as she faced Langley, who was just stepping out of the shower and now had no way to dry off.

"That's not fair." He glared, goose bumps rising on his arms from the cold air.

Jenna bit her lip; Langley watched her gaze as it meandered down his body, finally resting on his rock-hard erection. "I'm willing to share." She opened the towel teasingly, only allowing him a glimpse of the loveliness between her legs. Jenna wrapped the towel back around herself and turned toward the bedroom with a smirk.

She stopped before reaching the bed, Langley a step behind her. He put his palms on her shoulders and then brushed his fingertips down her arms. Langley turned his head to graze his lips against her neck, his hot breath eliciting a shiver.

He snaked an arm around and flicked loose the towel. Langley threw it on the bed as Jenna turned to face him.

"I want you, more than anything." She whispered, touching his chest gingerly.

Langley kissed her forehead, breathed in a familiar hint of lavender. For a brief moment, Langley's mind recounted the sound of squealing tires and his breath caught in his chest, but he was quickly brought back when Jenna put her warm hands on his muscled abs and glided them downward. Langley closed his eyes when Jenna delicately stroked the hard length of him and his legs trembled with anticipation.

As Jenna caressed him, she pulled him towards the bed

and sat down, her cheeks flushed. She scooted back as Langley put a knee on the bed between her legs.

He pushed his knee forward until it pressed against her and he could feel the heat of her sex against his leg. She laid herself down and wriggled backward to give him room; Langley climbed atop the bed, looking down at Jenna's wonderfully perky tits below him.

Langley ran his rough hand up her inner thigh while she squirmed. He inched the hand over her hip and onto her stomach as she trembled, her arms stretched above her head, breasts bouncing as she curved her body and moaned. As he leaned forward, he turned his arm and slid his hand down until his palm rested on her tight mound of curls.

She purred and pushed herself against his hand. Langley lowered himself to kiss her flexed stomach as she ran her fingers through his hair, softly passing his ears until she reached the stubble of his goatee. She rested her fingers on his lips as he raised his head to witness her parted lips and pleasured moans while he gently stroked her. Langley kissed her fingers softly as she sat up enough to look into his eyes.

Langley couldn't stop the smile that overtook him. Seeing Jenna squirm and pant at his touch was all that he had been craving; now that she'd finally made the choice to give herself over to him, body and mind, Langley wanted to ensure that this was a night she'd never forget.

Her freckled cheeks were rosy and she was incapable of lying still as Langley twirled her nipple between his fingers.

Langley slid his other hand further down until his palm rested on her clit, his finger slowly stroking the heat between her lower lips. He feared he might lose control of himself as she pressed herself against him with a whimper.

"David," she groaned breathlessly. With a sense of urgency, Jenna grabbed his neck and pulled him down on top of her. As Langley rested his chest on hers, she pushed her knee into his thigh and flipped him over onto his back, taking control.

Jenna lithely pounced atop him, her knees clenching his thighs. She bit her lip as she ran her hands down his muscled torso; Langley flexed against her hands as she got to his hips. She kneaded his quads as she rubbed herself on his leg. Langley thought he might erupt at the sight of her sitting on top of him.

"Do I need—"

Jenna shook her head. "I've got you. Trust me."

She grabbed him with one hand and stroked him; Langley clamped his hands onto the sides of her knees when Jenna twirled her finger around his head. Then she lifted her hips and put him inside of her, surrounding him in slick heat as she took his entire length in one motion.

Langley clenched his jaw, trying his best to hang on as his body already strained for release; Jenna was stroking his abs as she moved up and down, driving him wild. Langley grasped her hips as she started grinding against him, letting Jenna take the lead.

He was so wound up he knew he couldn't hold off long, especially as her tits bounced lavishly as she rode him. Langley slid his hand in between their bodies, his thumb rubbing her clit as she splayed her hands across his torso. She gasped at his touch and he knew she wasn't going to last long either. *Thank God.*

She arched her back and clutched his thighs, sweat dripping between her breasts.

"David!" She breathed. As her hips clenched, Langley drove upward as he massaged her harder. She shuddered and panted as she climaxed; Langley felt a surge of heat envelop him. Jenna quivered, leaning her head back as Langley pushed into her again, making her gasp. She squeezed him hard and Langley couldn't hold off any longer.

Jenna collapsed into his chest, wrapping her arms around his torso as her body continued to tremble. Langley hugged his arms around her and thrust into her further as he came, rocking her back and forth along his length while she dug her nails into his back.

Langley groaned aloud as he finished, his arms flexed around Jenna's tight body. He breathed deeply and let out a sigh as he closed his eyes, relishing the feeling of being inside of her. He loosened his grip and tried to catch his breath as he embraced her.

He kissed her damp hair, intoxicated by her sweetness. Langley moaned, finally feeling all of his muscles truly relax for the first time in what felt like forever. Langley's heart was thumping loudly in his own ears, and he could feel Jenna's chest heaving as she lay atop him. He ran a hand over her hair and along her back as she purred.

She rolled slightly and Langley grunted in sudden pain as she put her weight on his ribs. Langley lifted her up as he rolled out from underneath her, putting space in between them.

"Sorry!" She gently rubbed his injured ribs as he took a steadying breath. Langley leaned on an elbow and watched her long eyelashes as she looked over his torso.

"I'll get over it," he whispered with a smirk.

Jenna's smile was radiant and honest as she brought her gaze back to meet his. Dragging her hands coyly across his chest, she mirrored him and rested her head on a slender arm.

Langley put his hand on her ribs and slowly moved it down to her hips, loving the feeling of her soft skin beneath his hand. Jenna smiled as she snuggled her body against his, her breasts brushing against his chest. She draped an arm over his hip while Langley pulled the end of the blanket beneath them over Jenna's small frame. He slowly stroked her hair while she dragged her nails along his back.

"I don't want this to end." She whispered into his neck.

Langley kissed her softly on the cheek, pulling the blanket to cover his legs as well. Jenna turned so that their noses touched and he kissed her tenderly on the lips, staying silent. Langley felt her sigh into his chest as she pulled slightly away from him. He let her slide out of his arms but she stayed wrapped up next to him, her eyes focused on his.

"Are you ready to hear all of this? It might take a while." Jenna put a hand back onto Langley's chest.

"I'm sure we'll take breaks." He grinned broadly.

Jenna rolled her eyes as she playfully swatted his arm. "If you're up to it, that is."

Langley frowned. "Which, the talking or the breaks?"

Jenna squeezed his solid bicep with a sly smile. "Both." She moved up to his shoulder and he flexed beneath her touch. As Langley watched, Jenna's steely eyes lingered on his arms, then flicked to his chest. Finally she gazed up to see his roguish grin. She licked her lips while staring into his eyes, tilting her head to the side so that her hair cascaded down in front of her shoulder. Langley reached out and caressed her tits, felt them pebble beneath his touch.

"Enough talking, I'm ready for a break."

Jenna laughed. "You're joking. It's been, what, three minutes?"

Langley inhaled through his nose, shaking his head. Incredulously, Jenna swiped a hand down past his abs and

Langley delighted in the look of surprise that met Jenna's features when she reached between his legs.

As Jenna went to sit up, Langley grabbed her shoulder to stop her, his goatee tickling her cheek.

"My turn," he whispered, gently gesturing for her to lie back down.

Langley took his time this round. Starting at her slender legs, he gently massaged all the way up her lean body, savoring her moans and shivers as he rubbed her arms, shoulders, neck and then her breasts.

He tantalized her, leaving a trail of kisses starting at her neck and slowly inching their way down to her flexed stomach. Langley leisurely made his way down with his tongue until he was kissing her, tasting her as her fingers dug into his shoulders. He licked her gently, relishing her moans and tremors as she involuntarily stiffened beneath him. He teased her until she was hot, wet and flustered.

"*Dammit* David, I want you inside me already!" She growled, pulling his head up as he laughed.

Langley did as she requested; Langley pushed himself up onto his powerful arms. Jenna wrapped her legs around his hips as he slid inside of her, his arms bracing himself above her as he gently glided in and out. She was fighting Langley and kept trying to press herself hard against him and he shushed her, gently kissing her forehead as he slowed even more, drawing himself all the way out and back in again.

"You're torturing me," she whimpered after enduring a few more strokes, her legs squeezing around his hips as Langley chuckled.

He lowered himself to kiss her neck, then wrapped his arms all the way around her and pulled her up until they were both sitting upright, Jenna now straddled over his lap.

Langley grasped her ass as she rode him, her thighs trembling against his legs. She crushed her mouth against his, biting his lip and moaning into his mouth as she came for the second time.

Langley cherished the moment as she squeezed him in a bear hug, loving the feeling of her tightness around him as she convulsed in his arms. When her body finally relaxed, Langley nudged her back onto the bed. Her legs coiled around his hips once more as he gently pushed farther into her; she moaned as her eyes closed.

Lowering himself to his elbows so that his chest caressed her tits, he sped up the pace. She bucked her hips underneath him, letting Langley in deeper. With a grunt, Langley's hips seized as he came again, his torso rubbing against Jenna's soft skin while she squeezed her legs around him, taking him as deep as she could.

Langley's arms were shaking and he realized he couldn't hold himself up any longer. Utterly spent and exhausted, Langley unceremoniously rolled over and stared up at his ceiling as he breathed heavily, his ribs aching.

"Damn," Jenna whispered. "I've never came like that, twice in a row."

Langley laughed breathlessly. "Me neither."

CHAPTER EIGHTEEN

JENNA WAS EUPHORIC; not only was it the best sex of her life, but she had also freed her mind and given herself entirely to David, emotionally and physically. It was beyond liberating to have finally made that decision, though now the fear of the unknown consequences was starting to take root in her mind.

As he lay beside her, Jenna took a deep breath and shook her damp hair. Langley lazily turned his head to regard her. He looked far beyond merely tired; Jenna wasn't sure he'd make it through ten minutes of conversation with her. Although she didn't want the peaceful silence between them to end, she knew they needed to start talking before the sun came up—or before David passed out, which he looked on the brink of doing.

"Are you sure you want to do this right now?"

"Yes," he said, pushing himself up. He rubbed his face and shook his head vigorously back and forth.

Without preamble, Jenna started with her father's case: the police beating him in front of her and her brother, the rage and the aftermath of a harrowing, dragged-out court case. She told him how Frank had changed after that, how their mother had died of the stress and chaos of it all, how she'd joined the military to get away.

Langley seemed more alert the more she talked, and he didn't interrupt her except to occasionally brush a hair off of her face or stroke her arm. They stayed there wrapped in his blanket while Jenna talked.

"Then, the accident," Jenna found herself saying to him. He was nodding slowly. She recounted the surgeries on her leg, the plates and the pins required after the ridiculous Humvee crash during a boring training day in Afghanistan. "My father showed up once to the hospital in four months. Frank was there almost daily, helping me through." Jenna felt the tears welling. *And now I'm betraying him.*

"Jenna," it was the first time Langley had spoken since she'd started. "Your brother saved your sanity and probably your life, and you'll never forget that." He wiped a tear from her nose. "His bad choices now don't change how good he was to you then."

She nodded grimly. Jenna told him how she'd been hopeless and homeless and how Frank had taken her in. She'd stayed with her brother; he'd taken her to all of her rehab appointments, physical therapy and helped her get a job. And then Jenna told him how he'd started acting strange a few months ago, his cop-hating rage at an all-new high.

"He freaked out when he found out about your wreck and what I'd done to help. Says I should have left you there on the asphalt to die. After that point, he's been paranoid about my comings and goings since. He says he's trying to protect me by telling me to steer clear of you guys."

Langley rubbed his palms across his face. "I'm surprised he hasn't called you tonight wondering where you are."

Jenna felt her cheeks get hot. Her phone was in the car. "Uh..."

Langley looked at her despairingly and sighed. "You really are trying to get me killed."

"Not intentionally."

Langley slid off the bed and donned a pair of boxers. Jenna sat up, wrapping the blanket around her body.

"I don't know what my brother is doing, David. I know that he's up to something though, because his biker buddies are always over at the house creeping around. And Frank now keeps a pistol on him. That guy Rick is constantly coming and going, but he's very quiet."

Langley put on a tight black t-shirt, covering up his lovely abs. "Have you seen anything else unusual?"

Jenna shook her head. "I didn't even know Frank was involved with...whatever you're doing. They just sit in the garage and then go to the Saloon in the evenings, that's all I ever see them do."

"Thank you for being forthcoming, it's helpful."

"Why exactly *are* you investigating him?"

Langley put a hand on his hip. "Why do you think?" The question was asked softly.

Jenna sniffed. "I'm sure it's cars, drugs or guns."

Langley's only response was a nod and she realized he probably couldn't discuss the details with her.

"So, what do I do now? Do I just go home and pretend nothing happened? If he finds out I talked to the cops, or you, who knows what he'll do."

"Act normally. Go to work, stay away from your brother and his house as much as possible. It's all you can do until the investigation is over."

Jenna nodded. She stretched her arms over her head while Langley sat on the edge of the bed.

"And," Langley's voice was slightly gruff. "Plan on them having followed you here; I guarantee that Rick and your brother will test you. From what you've stated, Rick is very cautious and so is your brother. Don't lie, just remember this is *Dale's* apartment, and you spent the night with Dale."

Jenna frowned. "So, I spent the night with a druggie mechanic who has a girlfriend? My brother would never believe that."

Langley opened his arms wide, palms facing the ceiling. "There's no alternative. This is risky business. I never expected you to show up here, and we've got to deal with that now without blowing my cover, because if you blow my cover and your brother and his buddies find out, we're both in serious trouble."

"What about you? If you're right, they know where you live."

He shrugged. Jenna clicked her tongue in protest but Langley shook his head. "Don't worry about me, I'll be fine. It's you I'm worried about." His jaw clenched as he looked down at the floor. "I can't protect you from any of this when you leave here and that flat-out terrifies me, Jenna."

Jenna's eyebrows shot upward. She found it hard to believe that he could be terrified of anything, but his worried look made her smile broadly. "I'll make do. Besides, I've done nothing wrong."

"You're here with me." Langley's voice was gravelly, his look stern.

"Like you said, we have no choice. I'll do the best I can, lay low and stay out of the way until this is all over." Jenna bit her lip as David slowly nodded. She glanced outside; the night was still dark, but she knew that the dawn was not long behind.

She sighed. "You know my entire life story, and I know practically nothing about you. I know you were a Marine before you became a cop and I thought you might not make it that day of your wreck, but that's all I know."

Langley smiled as he rubbed his hand across the blanket that was draped over her legs. "I couldn't stand the thought of not seeing your face again, so dying wasn't an option once you showed up." Langley lifted his arms, palms open as he shook his head. "I'm not that interesting, I'm afraid. What is it you want to know?"

Jenna snorted. "You're the most ridiculously humble cop I've ever known."

"Don't tell my coworkers that, you'll blow my macho persona."

She laughed lightly and he smirked at her, sending her heart fluttering. "Seriously, at least tell me what your MOS was in the Corps."

His broad smile made Jenna's breath catch. "2676."

"Huh. I'd have guessed Recon or Military Police."

Langley barked a high-pitched laugh. "No, not me. I was a boring linguist in an office, that's it." He stooped his neck downward as he tugged at his shirt, looking over his shoulder at nothing. Jenna noticed his obvious discomfort as he added, "See? Not that interesting."

Jenna frowned at him as he slid around the bed; she started to ask another question but he deflected smoothly when he knelt down and grasped her hand within his.

"I'll tell you every uninteresting detail about my life after this investigation is over, I promise. Right now, though, I need to know—can you maintain my cover? Are you sure you'll be okay?" Langley's voice was deep and enchanting, making her forget about his former unease. Jenna never wanted to let go of his warm hands. She looked up at his chiseled jaw, his unwavering gaze.

"I'll do my best." Jenna squeezed his hands, then pushed herself off the bed as he stood beside her. "Is this it, then?"

Langley's shoulders drooped. He looked like death, his eyes bloodshot and his body fatigued. He took her into his arms, holding her in a tight embrace.

"You shouldn't come back here until this is over." He pushed his nose into her hair, gave her a kiss on top of the head. "Then, when it *is* over, there will be nothing to worry about and we'll continue what we started here tonight."

Jenna held him, loving his warmth and powerful presence. She felt safe there in his arms and she was terrified to leave. "I hope you're right."

As he swayed her gently, Jenna got a glimpse behind the bed.

"Alright, I have to ask one more question."

"What?"

"Why the hell is your only piece of décor in this barren place a cello?"

CHAPTER NINETEEN

LANGLEY SNORTED. "What do you have against my cello?"

"What exactly do you do with it?"

Langley frowned, pushing her shoulders back so that he could look at her face. "What the hell do you *think* I do with it?"

Jenna put both hands on his chest, eyebrow raised. "Wait. I'm sorry, *you* play it?"

Langley was rather insulted, and he let it show. Jenna giggled uncontrollably as she waved her hands in front of her face. "I just...can't. You, a Marine and a cop? Playing the cello?" She kept sniggering as she retrieved and started donning her clothes. "I don't believe it."

Langley shook his head dejectedly, glanced at his bedside clock. 4:07 am. *I've been up for thirty-three hours.* Langley sat down on the folding chair and turned the knob of the bow to tighten it while Jenna buttoned her pants. He fixed his gaze on his bow, his voice laced with sarcasm as he spoke.

"Let me guess: all Marines and cops are too busy flexing and posing in the mirror to manage having any other skills?"

Before she could consider responding, he bowed the strings to check the tuning then immediately started playing the last twenty measures of the Prelude of Bach's Cello Suite, one of his favorite solos. His hands were exhausted and it sounded like rubbish to his well-trained ears, but as he finished, Jenna covered her mouth with her hands, cheeks red.

"Oh my God!" She giggled hysterically, her eyes watering as she rocked back and forth on the bed, gasping between fits of laughter. "I think I just creamed in my pants."

Langley couldn't stop the booming laugh that overtook him. It felt so good to be so...*in love?* "Thank God, because if I tried to have sex right now, I'd die." He loosened the bow as she continued to laugh uncontrollably. He couldn't help but be swept up in her joy and he was grinning by the time she managed to catch her breath.

"I mean, you're *really* good. How in the hell does *this* not qualify as an interesting detail about your life?"

Langley snorted at her. "Alright, fine. My father was a lead cellist for a...very prominent orchestra. It seemed fitting that his only son would attempt to live up to the standard." Langley brooded a moment as he leaned the cello back onto the chair.

When he turned, he was bombarded by Jenna as she leapt off the bed and threw her arms around him. Jenna hugged him tight, slender arms around his neck. She gave him a kiss on the cheek and bounced away from him just as quickly, a wonderfully bright smile on her face. Her pure happiness made Langley grin with sudden cheerfulness, momentarily forgetting the stress of the investigation.

"You're the only man I've ever known that can make me feel completely amazing while also making me feel like a total jerk." She shook her head while her blue eyes stayed focused on Langley. "I hope this is all over soon, David, because I want a lot more of you. And I want a *lot* more of that cello."

With another giggle, she skipped out of the room and stopped at the front door.

"Jenna," Langley whispered as he followed, putting his hand on the knob. The first light of the day was just glimmering on the horizon. "Be careful."

"I will, David." She bit her lip, gazed into his eyes. "You...well, I mean, I—"

He reached out and squeezed her hand, ending her stammering.

"The feeling is mutual, Jenna." He said quietly before she could say anything else. Jenna blinked at him, then crushed her mouth against his, her hand gliding across the back of his neck before she quickly pulled away. Her lips trembled as he opened the door; she slipped away, disappearing into the shadows.

Langley barely made it back to the bed before he collapsed, surrendering to a deep, peaceful sleep.

Langley thought he was dreaming when he heard his cover phone ringing. Groggy, he groped around and rolled off the bed onto his knees to find it discarded on the floor. He barely made out the time before he answered it with a grunt. 7:47 am.

"Uh, Dale." There was an ungodly amount of stammering from Barnes as she told him to come to the cover house for breakfast and a meeting with the team.

Three hours of sleep was not enough to recover from the night's events; Langley tried to stretch away the stiffness in his muscles while dragging himself off the floor. He took a shower, dressed in more ragged clothes with his concealed revolver at his back and got on his low rider, hoping the breeze in his face would wake him up on the ride over. Images of Jenna laughing played through his mind, making him smile broadly beneath his bandana.

When Langley arrived at the house, Barnes was outside to meet him.

"Hey Bailey," he said for aesthetics. She was silent, a cup of coffee in her hands that she seemed to be studying intently. "Is everything okay?" Langley realized she was alarmingly quiet.

All she did was shake her head, refusing to look at him.

She went inside and immediately disappeared around the corner. Carlson was sitting at a card table with ear phones in, his face a deep color of crimson as he fiddled with something in his lap. Miller was rubbing his mouth briskly, looking down at some papers. Harris was smothering what appeared to be either a laugh or a cough, Langley couldn't tell which, and Keene was the only one staring straight at Langley's face, an asshole smirk on his lips.

"Hungry?" Keene asked. Harris snorted into his hand and swiftly exited the room. Carlson cleared his throat, still looking down.

Langley regarded all of them in turn, trying to decipher the obvious and awkward dynamic in the room. He took the offered fast food bag from Keene and inhaled the contents in less than thirty seconds, not even bothering to sit down.

"Uh, Langley," Keene started to say, his hands in front of him as Langley threw the bag in the trash can next to Carlson. Miller had stood up from his perch and also had his hands casually in front of him. Langley knew their stances all too well.

Langley felt his hackles rise.

"Dude," Harris chuckled as he came back from the other room, his FBI badge flashing under his suit coat. He moved to stand beside Keene, his hands on his hips and a look of brotherly respect on his face. "You're a *beast*, man."

Langley was confused. "Huh?"

Miller seemed unable to help himself as he chortled. "And how come you never told anyone you could play the cello?"

CHAPTER TWENTY

IT TOOK ONLY A MOMENT for realization to set in. When it did, Langley saw nothing but red. Before he could control himself, he was diving for Keene's throat.

They had expected it, obviously, as suddenly there were three people on top of him and one knew just where to thump him on his ribs to make him stop resisting.

With his face smashed to the hard wood floor and limbs splayed beneath the bulk of three men, Langley growled a string of colorful curses before spluttering out something coherent.

"Show me the warrant for tapping my apartment!"

All six hands released him and Langley pushed himself into a sitting position on the floor. Keene handed him a sheet of paper as if he'd expected the question.

"You are really good, by the way." Keene waggled a finger at him. Miller guffawed at the connotation before Keene clarified. "On eliciting information, I mean." Langley wanted to gouge the sick smile off of Keene's face. He thought he might throw up as he realized everything that the whole team had heard from the night before.

"Why?" Langley looked to Miller as he stood, feeling

the ultimate sense of betrayal from a man he thought was his brother-in-arms.

Miller sighed. "Sorry, Lang. Your girl lives with a main person of interest in this case." Miller nodded towards Keene and Harris. "These guys have been tracking her since she called you at the station. I was only brought in after the phone tap mix-up with Carlson." Miller sat down on the edge of a weathered desk, looking at his boots. "When you start having phone conversations—and lying to me about them in front of my face—we are obligated to find out what you're really up to."

"You could have just *asked!*" Langley shouted, throwing his arms up in the air.

Keene shook his head. "You're lucky. We believed Jenna was running you for Frankie P-Pat York, her brother." Keene came to stand in front of Langley, his eyes looking slightly up to meet Langley's fierce glare. "She could have blown your cover. Or worse, she could have set you and all of us up and gotten someone killed. We were protecting you." Keene switched back to prick-mode, a boorish grin covering his face. "But hey, thanks for working her for *everything* she had to offer." He sniggered as he bobbled his head. Langley barely restrained from slamming a fist into him as he continued. "You were right, by the way; her brother already knows about her being with you last night. So now you've got to account for your alter-ego screwing her while you're supposed to be with Bailey over there."

Langley digested the speech. "Acknowledged. Now get the bug out of my apartment."

"No problem." Keene shrugged. "Because you're now assigned a 24-hour wire until this is over."

Langley glowered, fighting the overwhelming urge to scream. "I'm already on board. You know Jenna's innocent, there's nothing more to get there."

"Actually," Keene strained his neck forward, fiddling with his shirt collar. "She's not entirely innocent. Frank had her car packed full of meth last night at the party. And she was the transporter that drove it back to her brother's house for safekeeping, right before she took off for your place."

"What are you saying?" Langley did not appreciate the dance that Keene was doing with his words.

"We'll charge her with it if she doesn't agree to turn."

Langley's mouth dropped. "She's not a rat!"

"Sure as hell sounded like she was ratting last night, Detective." Keene sneered back. "She needs to come in so we can have her start snooping and plant two mics on some bikes, then she'll be free and clear. She's got to help nab two in exchange for her to walk, and we've already started the groundwork for her."

"No." Langley snapped, his temper flaring as his protectiveness went into overdrive.

Keene stepped closer, getting inches from Langley's face.

"I don't care who you fuck, Langley, but I care if it *fucks with my case!*" Keene snarled, jabbing his finger into Langley's chest. "She gets on board, or you both hang— obstruction for you and accomplice for her."

"Do not involve her. She doesn't need to know any of this." Langley fumed. "I'll plant the mics for her."

"Lang, that's insane, I won't allow you to get yourself killed—" Miller started to interject.

"I don't care how it gets done," Keene barked, turning his back on Langley as he sauntered toward Carlson's table. "But Rick and Frank are what I want in exchange for her. Those two are elusive and easily spooked. They hide their phones and they don't talk in Frank's garage. I know Rick is more than what he seems." Keene turned again and extended a hand toward Langley, one large microphone and two tiny wireless microphones resting in his palm. "If you're foolish enough to risk your cover, your job and your life to plant these when she could just do it while they sleep, be my guest. But I refuse to risk my whole operation for your ass, so you'd better have a damn good plan."

Jaw clenched, Langley snatched the three microphones; he clipped the larger one deep inside his shirt and pocketed the two smaller ones.

"Uh, guys?" Carlson's meek voice made everyone turn as he lowered his headphones. "They're across the street."

Keene made an exasperated face at Carlson. *"Who?"*

"Sorry. Frank and Rick. They are sitting at some guy named Chuckie's place waiting for Dale—er, Detective Langley. Frank just...um..." Carlson's eyes flitted between Keene and Langley.

"Carlson, just say it." Langley put his hands on his hips as he relaxed his own stance, brushing at the floor with his boot. "My loyalty is to the op, first and foremost."

Miller nodded approval before Carlson continued.

"Frank called Jenna, told her to stay away from Dale because he's a low-life druggie. Then he told someone else that he'd handle the rest."

Langley let his chin drop and took a deep breath. Keene threw his arms up in the air as he turned and faced Carlson's desk.

"Christ!" Keene barked. "Could you possibly have screwed this up any more, Detective?" Keen spun on his heels and stomped towards Langley. "I would pull you out now, but you're too far in and we're too close. What do you propose we do about *this?*" Keene's bladed hand shook as he gestured to the street out the window.

"What are the options?" Langley opened his arms. "Running would only aggravate them and take focus off the task at hand. A little threatening or bruising isn't worth blowing my cover or the op." Langley rested his hands low on his hips as he matched Keene's fierce glare. "I'll take it, unless they pull weapons. I'll plant these, too." Langley shrugged as he tapped his pocket.

"Goddamn," Harris' eyebrows shot up as he rubbed his chin. "After listening to everything last night and seeing you today, I've no doubt you are class-one in *love* with this broad if you're willing to get your ass whooped for a mere chance at wiring those guys for her."

Langley regarded him coolly. "I'll consider the ass whooping a penance for unintentionally causing this mess in the first place."

Miller whipped his phone out of his pocket as he pointed at Langley. "Hide your piece. I'll stage a beat cop close by; if they get too rough I'll have them light you up and intervene." Miller glowered at Langley. "If it gets too heavy, say so and we'll get you the hell out."

Carlson was back on the headphones and he pulled out two pieces of paper from the printer. "Warrants for the taps and GPS," he handed the sheets to Keene.

"With them being right across the street, how do you propose we do this?" Miller asked, eyes shifting from Langley to Keene.

Langley laughed even though his hands had started to shake from the adrenaline now pulsing through him. "Hey, Barnes?"

"Yeah Lang."

"Let's give everyone a good show."

It took five minutes to stage Langley's exit and make

sure all Miller's logistics were in order so that cops would be able to jump in at a moment's notice if things got out of hand. Langley had his small revolver now attached to the inside of his boot and had his route planned for getting home. He staged the two small microphones inside the cuff of his shirt so that they were easily accessible. Barnes was grabbing some random household items sitting around: a toaster, a coffee pot and a curling iron. She started screaming curses before Langley flung open the door to the duplex.

"You lying, no-good, cheatin' *bastard!*" Barnes screeched, launching the toaster out the front door.

Langley stumbled and crashed into the planter out front, ducking as the coffee pot came hurdling over his head next.

"Babe, I'm sorry—"

"Get outta my house!"

Langley hopped onto his motorcycle as the cord of the curling iron whacked him in the face. With a roar, Langley kicked off the asphalt and steered his low rider onto the residential street, slapping his helmet on his head as he shifted gears.

He wasn't sure where exactly Frank was or what he was planning, but if it was just a little bruising, Langley could handle that. *Tough big brother 'protecting' his little sister,* Langley mused. *I almost feel bad for the naïve bastard.* As he pulled up to a red light, he could hear the engine of at least one distant motorcycle.

Casually, Langley acted as if he were heading back to his place on the side streets. He saw a patrol car parked at a coffee house and could see someone sitting in the driver's seat on the phone. *Hello, back-up.*

Langley stopped again at a stop sign, lingering and

taking his time before revving his bike. As he'd predicted, two motorcycles pulled up behind him. As Langley shifted hard to speed up, one of the bikes roared right past him, pacing ahead until an alley came up; the bike ahead of him abruptly turned left, forcing Langley to do the same to avoid a collision.

Cranking the handlebars to the left, Langley skidded into an alleyway full of business dumpsters. Frank had cut him off and was hovering in front; Rick had pulled up right alongside Langley's bike and then Langley heard the sound of a third behind him.

Shit.

Frank slammed on the brakes and jumped off when they were halfway into the alley; Rick grabbed Langley's hand on the handlebars and practically crushed it as he forced Langley off the throttle. The third bike pulled alongside him and Langley didn't recognize the gaunt man.

"Hey man, what the hell!" Although Langley knew he could probably take on all three of them if he had to, even in his current condition, he feigned weakness and meekly fought against Rick's death grip.

"Kill it, bitch." Frank barked, now standing beside Langley's bike. In a swift motion, both beefy men had vice grips on Langley's arms.

They dragged Langley off his bike, sending it crashing to the ground in the deserted alley. Langley kicked Rick in the shin which was reciprocated by a knee to the gut. As Langley doubled over, Frank's place was taken by the third lanky biker and Langley's arms were ratcheted behind his back, his shoulders straining against their hold. Frank now stood before him, steel eyes glowering as he snarled at Langley.

"Dale, was it?"

Langley sneered at Frank and started to curse at him, fighting against the men holding his arms.

Frank took the opportunity to land a solid punch straight into Langley's face. Langley felt a gush of warmth as his lip ruptured between his tooth and Frank's fist; the entire lip went numb instantly.

"Lowlife user. Stay the hell away from my sister!" Frank's blue eyes were vicious as he spat in Langley's face.

"Fff—" As Langley started to speak, he inadvertently sprayed blood all over Frank's face.

Frank drove a fist straight into Langley's ribs followed quickly by a punch to the gut, completely shutting him down. Langley sank back into Rick as his legs gave out, but Rick and the lanky man held him upright. *Jesus, why is it always the ribs?*

Frank flung open the sides of Langley's jacket, swiped a hand across his chest and shirt pockets as Langley groaned.

"This is your only warning."

Langley was watching his blood splatter onto the asphalt as it dripped off his chin. Rick abruptly released him, causing Langley to fall to his knees. As they triumphantly strolled back toward their bikes, Langley slid the two microphones out, placing one in each of the palms of his hands. He wiped the blood from his face with the back of his right hand and took a shaky breath.

"Frank!" Langley called out, stumbling behind them. They all turned in that instant to watch him as he clutched his side with his bloody hand, stooped over and looking pathetic as he staggered towards them. "I'll make sure my cousin hears about this!"

Frank's eyebrows danced upward as he watched Langley approach. "I don't give a damn." Frank pounded his fists together while turning to continue the last few steps to the line of bikes.

Langley cursed at him again and Frank turned to glare. Langley spit some blood out of his mouth, still stumbling after them. *Just a few more steps...*he spouted off the first thing that came to his mind in the hopes of making Frank pause once more.

"You came onto my girl at that party, Frank!"

The lanky man was standing in front of him, arms up as if he were going to swing. He was standing between Langley and the two bikes that were in line with Langley's fallen bike.

Langley dropped the stumbling act and drove his shoulder straight into the biker, sending him sprawling backwards to collide with one of the motorcycles. The man and the bike both crashed down to the asphalt, filling the alleyway with resonating sounds of clanging metal.

As Langley went to jump over the bike, he slapped his right hand underneath the frame near the rear tire and felt the satisfying thud of the tiny microphone as it left his hand.

Rick was at the other bike, fists raised. With curses flying and the sudden roar of one of the motorcycles, the noise was amplified further by the siren of a cop car. Langley dove over his fallen bike and into Rick, grunting as he took a knee to the chest. Rick was more adept than the lanky man, so Rick barely knocked into his own motorcycle as Langley collided with him.

Using his shoulder, Langley spun Rick a bit so that he could reach his left hand down, feinting a fall, and slapped the microphone underneath the front of the frame.

Langley didn't expect the knee to the collarbone and was forcefully driven straight back into his own fallen motorcycle, the impact of the blow causing his bike to scrape on the asphalt as his body collided with it. The deafening roar of bikes drowned out all noise as the three bruisers revved their engines.

Choking on blood, Langley sank back into his fallen motorcycle as he watched the three bikers skid out of the alley, a patrol car approaching quickly from the other direction.

Chest heaving, Langley replayed the action in his mind. Then he realized his grave mistake.

"No!" Langley slapped his hands over his eyes. As the noise of the bikes disappeared and the cop cut the siren, he slid his hands back to grasp his temples as he snarled aloud in frustration, sending a slew of bloody spit splattering onto the ground. Langley spoke to his team through his hidden microphone, knowing they were all at the edge of their seats on the other end.

"Dammit, *I got the wrong bike!*"

CHAPTER TWENTY ONE

JENNA WAS LEAVING THE DINER, closing out another day full of jerks and scant tips. She'd already been threatened by her brother that morning as she arrived at work, and it had set her up for an awful day.

After stripping off her apron, Jenna was about to stroll through the front door when she saw a fidgety man of maybe twenty-two bee-bopping by the entryway. Jenna frowned and slowed her walk as she tried to circumnavigate him to get through the door.

"Hi." He said to her, his cheeks suddenly red. Jenna narrowed her eyes at the boy, swaggering right by him to get out. "Whoa! Wait a sec," he said quietly, following right behind her as she exited the diner.

She sniffed in annoyance while continuing to walk away. "What do you want?"

His gaze bounced all over the parking lot as he leaned close to her ear, stumbling to keep up. "It's about Detective Langley." He whispered. Jenna abruptly stopped walking and the man bumped into her with a mumbled apology.

Jenna blinked. "Who are you?"

"I'm Carlson." He waved to her awkwardly even

though he was standing a foot away. Jenna raised an eyebrow at him, wondering if he was just pretending to be foolish or if that's how he actually *was*. Jenna stayed silent and waited for him to explain himself. "Sorry. Well, he—we—need your help. You see that green sedan under the tree at the back of the parking lot?"

Jenna kept her head trained on the boy Carlson, but her eyes found the green car.

"Just get in and he'll explain everything."

A patron of the diner came out, excusing himself as he passed between them.

"Thanks." Carlson's cheeks went red as he sauntered off, hands stuffed in his pockets.

My help with what? Jenna looked around the parking lot and immediately headed towards the car.

When she reached the passenger door, she popped it open and slid in, expecting David to be in the driver's seat as she shut the car door.

It wasn't.

"Hello, Jenna." The man rubbed his chin briskly. "My name is Lieutenant Miller."

Jenna had the handle half pulled to exit the vehicle when the man named Miller put a hand on her shoulder. She froze; he wasn't restraining her, but she could sense the anxiety in his touch. Glancing back at his face proved her assessment to be correct as his eyes were plagued with worry.

"Don't worry, no one knows you're here."

Jenna inhaled sharply. "I'm only here because Carlson said that David needed help."

Miller's lips tightened and a tiny sigh escaped from the corner of his mouth. "He does." With a shake of his head, Miller dropped his hand back to the center divider of the car, leaning a bit towards Jenna. "You know what your brother is up to and you're aware that Detective Langley is working on the case."

Jenna nodded once, wondering how much more Lieutenant Miller knew.

Miller rubbed his forehead, sighing before speaking. "Langley is my best detective. He's one of the finest, most honorable men I've ever worked alongside. I trust him with my life." Miller took a steadying breath while leveling his gaze on Jenna's eyes. "I believe you trust him as much as I do, and I think we both are doing everything possible to protect him while this investigation is ongoing."

"Yes." Jenna answered slowly.

"Then I need you to do me a small favor."

Jenna tilted her head slightly, waiting for the Lieutenant to continue.

He opened his hand and produced what looked like a small string attached to a box no bigger than a lip balm. "Do you know what this is?"

"No."

"It's a wireless microphone. I need you to put this on your brother's motorcycle."

Jenna's breath caught in her chest. "I can't."

Miller shifted in his seat and looked out the windshield, letting the silence hang for a moment. "Your brother called you this morning. He told you to stay away from Dale, whom your brother doesn't know is Detective Langley, right?"

Jenna's mouth opened to answer, and then she realized what he was actually stating. "You're listening to our phone conversations?"

Miller nodded curtly. "Did you hear what your brother said at the end of the call, right before he hung up?"

Of course she'd heard. She hadn't known what Frank was implying, but Jenna's heart started racing as she answered. "He said he'd handle it."

"That's correct." He leaned across the center of the car, his head lowering as he locked his gaze with Jenna's. "Did you know that your brother and his biker buddies beat the living shit out of Langley this morning? Langley was adamant that I allow it to happen. He took the beating without defending himself because he was trying to do this—" Miller waved the microphone "—just so that I wouldn't ask *you* to."

Jenna's hands flew to her mouth; she saw a slight mist in Miller's focused eyes.

"Look, David would do goddamn *anything* right now to protect you from everyone, biker and cop alike, but I really don't want him to fucking *die* in the process." Miller cleared his throat. "Jenna—"

"Nothing more needs to be said, Lieutenant." Jenna stated firmly as she took the microphone from Miller's hand. She narrowed her eyelids knowingly. "I have no doubt that you already know whose side I'm on. Just tell me what you need me to do."

Langley had been put on strict orders from Lieutenant Miller to go the hell home and tend to the six new stitches in his lip. He'd gotten an earful from Miller and Keene over the beat cop's phone for his stunt. After a stop at the ER for stitches and pain killers, Langley was actually looking forward to lying low until things calmed down.

The tapping of the wrong bike took time to sort out as the team had to scramble for the proper paperwork to support probable cause on one Chuckie Foster, but in the end they had gotten what they needed.

Except Frank. That was a complete failure.

Cursing as he stepped out of a long shower, Langley was still fuming over his mistake. Miller had been abundantly clear, however: Langley was not allowed to go anywhere near Jenna or Frank until the sting was over, so Langley wasn't sure how they were going to fix his screw-up. For now, Langley would take Miller's advice and stay out of the limelight.

After doubly checking to be certain his doors and windows were locked, Langley staged one pistol under his pillow while his revolver stayed holstered and attached to him as he collapsed on the bed, the afternoon sun shining mercilessly through his blinds.

Langley passed out just after he glanced at the clock: 12:32 PM.

Drenched in cold sweat, Langley sprang awake at the sound of a blaring car horn. He groped for his revolver as he opened his eyes, clearing his entire apartment before taking a normal breath.

His lip was still aggravatingly numb and the stitches were throbbing ceaselessly. The pain, however, did not diminish how incredibly hungry Langley felt. The sun had lightened a bit, but was still shining through his blinds.

As Langley dressed himself in his Dale get-up with the intent to go get a bite to eat, his cover phone rang.

"Dale," he said, even though the number was Barnes'.

"Hey, come over when you get a chance. Plan on staying a while."

Langley snorted. "I just left. Miss me already?"

There was a pause. "You were here yesterday."

"No, I..." Langley stopped, his brow furrowed. He looked at his clock: 9:01 AM. *I just slept for an entire day.*

"Damn. Ok, I'll see you soon."

After attempting to eat a meal while navigating his swollen lip, Langley bitterly rode his motorcycle over to the cover house, duffel bag of his basic necessities in tow. Barnes gave him the thumbs up that no one was following him and he sauntered into the duplex, dropping his bag against the wall while she closed the door behind him.

"Langley," Miller barked when Barnes locked the front door. "You are not allowed to get hit, punched, run over or otherwise injured until after this operation is over, do you understand?"

Langley nodded as his eyebrow shot up.

"You're restricted to the desks and the only permissible injury is a paper cut. Am I clear?"

"Yes, sir."

"Wonderful. Turn in your wire and pull up a chair, because we've got a lot to do and I'm tired of listening to you snore."

Langley handed his microphone over and was quite content to be confined to a desk.

Barnes slipped out to handle errands for Miller while Langley started tackling the backlog of administrative tasks and general logistics that had fallen by the wayside when everyone on his team got assigned out of the office; Carlson had been doing it by himself with only minor assistance from Barnes and he wasn't efficient enough to keep up, especially since he was new to the unit. Langley quickly took the lead and Carlson was happy to finally have a dedicated mentor. Langley was moderately surprised that Carlson wasn't his usual, annoying self; he was actually performing as an asset to the team.

By the time the sun started going down, there was much less tension in the duplex and everyone was genuinely relaxed for the first time since the Feds came on board.

"I think I need to assign you to admin more often." Miller smiled wickedly, handing Langley a wrapped sandwich just as Langley finalized the last report to send out to the Task Force.

"Not funny." Langley glared. "Hey," Langley turned to Miller, a thought coming to him. "Where the hell is Neil?"

"He got his foot into the gang as some sort of bodyguard, which fits. He's doing a hell of a lot better than you at this point. Keene runs him, but he still briefs me once in a while. I'll certainly be sure to brief him on all of this when I talk to him." Miller winked at Langley.

Langley grimaced as he took a bite of his sandwich, feeling needles in his lip as Keene and Harris packed up their equipment. When Keene finished gathering his gear, he stood before the three men of the Brookside PD.

"Looks like we're closing in, gents." Keene set a briefcase down with a clunk on the hardwood floor. "The rest of the Feds are setting up with us at the motel and the final showdown should happen within the next two weeks."

Miller, Langley and Carlson all nodded as one.

"Miller, Greer is the linchpin and has to remain under the jurisdiction of the Task Force. You can shadow him but I call the shots." Keene waved a finger, passing from Carlson to Langley then resting on Miller. "Your team here remains in charge of Danny, Frank York and Rick; if you identify more targets through their wires, just pass them my way because I've got thirty more personnel to task out." Keene jabbed a thumb in Langley's direction while looking at Miller. "Figured lover boy over here would appreciate that."

Langley crossed his arms over his broad chest and leaned back in his desk chair, bouncing on his toes to recline the seat. "And all this time I thought you despised me."

Keene barked a laugh. "No Detective, I genuinely admire your noble stupidity, general selflessness and gung-ho motivation. Especially when it involves you getting beat up on a daily basis." Langley stomped his boots on the ground but Keene waved his hands in front of himself with a chuckle before Langley could speak. "Pipe down, Detective. I don't know many agents who could pull off the shit you have in the past few months, maintain their cover and live to tell the tale. You should consider a future with the FBI when this is over."

Now it was Langley's turn to laugh. "I'll pass, thanks."

"Suit yourself." Keene shrugged. "Miller, we'll conference every shift change."

"Roger."

Keene picked up the briefcase and headed for the door.

Harris tossed his head as a goodbye to everyone in the room, then looked at Langley before following Keene out the door. "Semper."

"'Rah." Langley responded with a respectful nod.

The door closed and Miller let out a heavy sigh.

"What?" Carlson scratched his head and looked at Langley.

Langley eyed Carlson but Miller responded first.

"Marines." Miller waved his hand dismissively. "They speak their own language."

"Hey, wait a second." Langley ignored Carlson and turned his fierce glare to Miller as he leaned forward in the chair. "Frank's wired?"

Miller matched the glare, both hands on his hips. "Yes, Langley, Jenna did it and your objections are overruled."

Langley growled, shoving the chair backwards into the wall as he stood. "I—"

"Drop it, Lang! Jenna understood the risks when she made the choice to do it, and we both know she's capable of maintaining secrecy and handling herself."

Langley's nostrils flared as Miller continued.

"I've allowed you to get away with a lot of shit regarding her and I put my own neck out there during the FBI's investigation of you two. You did all you could to keep her out of this." Miller flung his arms out wide. "There were no other options, Langley! We needed it done. In the end, she chose *you* over her own goddamn family. She's devoted to you just as much as you are to her and this whole operation. So get the hell over it, let's get through this thing safely, then you can—how did you put it? 'Continue what you started' with her?"

Langley's lips were taut as he regarded Miller.

"Relax, Langley." Miller sat down on one of the desks. "Even if Frank found the mic and spooked, what would he do? Accuse Jenna?"

"I don't know," Langley admitted. "And not knowing is what I fear the most."

CHAPTER TWENTY TWO

DAYS OF MONOTONY PASSED until the numerous teams of the task force were each gathered in their separate hideouts, listening in on Greer's current conversation with Red and a number of other drug dealers. Everyone was collectively holding their breath while gathering around their respective computer screens.

When Langley heard the thud of Greer's hand connect with Red's over the airwaves, everyone started rejoicing. Greer had pulled it off: he had set up the deal to buy an exorbitant amount of meth and heroin. With the FBI tracking most of the network, the task force would wait, watch and gather evidence as the drugs passed between hands. By the time the exchange with Greer was set to go down, there would be about forty arrests and at least three residences involved in the multi-agency raid.

One residence, of course, was Frank York's house. The evidence compiled was now just enough to prosecute; thanks to Langley and Jenna, the bike wires had provided some audio evidence to charge Rick and Frank, who drove far outside the city limits to talk shop. It gave Langley only slight comfort to know that Jenna wasn't privy to how cunning her brother really was.

Langley was on edge every day, listening in on the bland conversations over the microphones and occasionally hearing Jenna's voice as she nonchalantly chatted with her brother. He couldn't remember the last time his palms *weren't* clammy. Langley desperately wanted this all to be over and wondered if Jenna was as terrified as he was.

Langley was sitting at one of the desks with a set of headphones on, monitoring Rick as he talked about a football game in someone's garage. Given the constant static of road noise that had been activating the microphone, the batteries were certainly set to die soon and Langley was hoping to find out more before that happened. While Langley listened, Carlson was forwarding targets to Keene and Miller was listening in on Greer. Barnes and a group of FBI agents were out driving cars close to Rick and the other bikers' locations to provide the wireless relay for the wires.

"Well, it sounds like your baffles are loose." Someone was saying.

"No kidding?" Rick's voice. *"Thought that asshole was lying."*

Langley snorted to himself as tools started banging around on the bike. He'd started to tune out their general mechanic talk and was chatting with Miller. The sun was just beginning to set and it was casting a yellow glow inside the duplex. There was excessive shuffling and scraping sounds over Rick's microphone.

And then Langley froze in his chair.

Miller immediately noticed the change in Langley's demeanor. "What?"

Langley ripped out the headphones, cranked up the volume and shushed everyone.

"What the hell is that?" Rick's voice was saying.

"That has nothing to do with your electrical." The other voice said.

"Oh shit." Miller couldn't dial his phone fast enough.

"It's not hooked to anything. Is that...holy shit!" Rick barked. There was loud scratching and a ripping noise. Agonizing seconds of silence went by. Then, *"Frank? I told you this was coming."*

"Jesus, Keene, answer your phone!" Miller panicked.

They heard a resonating *clang*. Then the microphone went dead.

Jenna was merely existing, going through the motions, being bland and passive while her insides constantly turned in knots with fear. She hadn't been contacted by anyone else after her one conversation with Lieutenant Miller; a lack of information didn't help her anxiety as she had no idea when the operation would be over or what was actually going on.

Placing the microphone on the frame of Frank's bike was the easy part; Jenna hadn't been prepared for the psychological consequences. She had constant nightmares and near-panic attacks at the thought of Frank discovering it. Sometimes she dreamt of Frank hunting down David Langley and it would cause her to wake up gasping for air. It was wreaking havoc on her internally, even more than the turmoil of her father's case had a decade ago. Pretending to be normal had never been so unnerving, and she always felt as if Frank's eyes were boring straight into her, seeing through her lies and uncovering the truth Jenna kept so carefully guarded.

Frank had only once brought up her night spent with 'Dale', and when Jenna had dismissed it as nothing more than a one night stand, he'd never brought it up again. But he had certainly been much more scrutinizing ever since, and Jenna constantly felt as if there were eyes on her all the time.

Jenna wanted nothing more than to have David's arms around her again, feel him hold and comfort her. She oft found herself daydreaming about his sensual kisses, his humbleness and his enigmatic past that he downplayed so smoothly. *Soon, Jenna. Once this is over...*

She was leaving for the store, keys in hand, when she heard her brother answer his phone in the living room. "What's up Rick," he was saying.

As she opened the garage door, she heard her brother let out a string of loud profanity.

"A wire?" He growled between swearing.

Jenna was midstride and heading out of the garage door when she reacted, balking so violently that she tripped and crashed down to her knees on the garage floor, keys skittering while the door slammed against the wall with a resonating thud.

No! Jenna got one foot underneath her as she looked towards Frank's bike, impulsiveness guiding her.

Jenna dove head first, sliding across the garage floor until she collided with her brother's motorcycle. While still in motion, Jenna grabbed the sticky microphone with both hands and prayed her brother wouldn't come through the door as she manically yanked at it.

Three pulls later it was free; Jenna rolled away from the motorcycle, shoving the microphone down her pants where it stuck to the inside of her jeans. She had enough time to sit up before her brother flew into the garage wielding his cell phone. Jenna rocked back and forth on the ground while holding her formerly injured leg, genuine tears in her eyes.

"Where!" Frank screamed. He started frantically

skimming his hands along his bike frame. Jenna didn't dare breathe as Frank took the five seconds to swipe his whole bike. "There's nothing here." Frank paused as he listened to Rick; Jenna whimpered, still swaying on the ground as she clenched her teeth dramatically, letting the tears flow freely. "Ok, ok."

Suddenly, Frank's eyes locked onto Jenna and she felt like prey in the crosshairs. The coldness Jenna saw there produced a wave of fear that made her hold her breath.

"Yes. I understand." Frank said calmly. He hung up the phone without altering his gaze, and the scrutiny made Jenna swallow hard.

Frank held out one hand, slowly panning his arm around the garage. "What the hell are you doing in here?"

Jenna exaggerated a sob. "I tripped and hit my leg, Frank." She wiped a hand under her nose as she closed her eyes and took a deep breath, wanting to break his steely glare. "I was going to the store."

Slowly, she turned her face towards her brother as she opened her eyes. His face was changing from red to white as he stared at her, his hand crushing his cell phone while he breathed shallowly.

"Are you okay?" Jenna asked him with a sniff. "What's going on?"

Frank sneered in response. He quickly bent and retrieved Jenna's keys, jamming them into his own pocket.

"You're not going anywhere." Frank's voice was ice.

"What?" Jenna blinked.

"Don't play stupid. You know too much. Call off work, now, then give me your phone."

"Frank, I—"

"Don't argue!" Frank bellowed as he covered the ground between them. He stood above her as she cowered

on the floor. "Do it."

Jenna hesitated. Frank suddenly reached inside of his vest and rested his hand on the grip of a pistol protruding from the waistband of his jeans.

"I said do it. *Now.*"

CHAPTER TWENTY THREE

LANGLEY'S HANDS WERE trembling as he listened to Jenna and Frank go back and forth, the sound now slightly muffled from whatever had transpired with the wire in the garage. Rick's phone call to Frank had been far too cryptic for them to deduce anything, but Langley's team knew that everything involved with the investigation was in the process of imploding. They all realized that Jenna must have removed the microphone when Frank couldn't find it, but they hadn't a clue what she'd done with it. Miller and Carlson were captivated, hovering around the desk while Langley shifted anxiously behind them.

"You're not going anywhere."

"To hell with that!" Langley shouted, rushing to the front door.

Miller pounced on his back, cell phone in hand.

"Wait!" Miller yelled, boots dragging on the floor as Langley's momentum hurtled him forward. "Jesus, Langley, have you lost your mind? You're thinking with the wrong head! *Wait!*"

"Wait for *what?* Miller, he's kidnapping her!" Langley dipped his shoulder and Miller pitched forward. As Miller stumbled, Langley grabbed Miller's shirt collar and rammed him into the wall of the duplex. "I can't just sit here and let this happen!" Langley abruptly released his hold and grabbed his own temples with trembling hands. "Now that they know we're on to them, we could lose track of them within minutes. We can't lose them, Miller. *I* can't lose her."

Miller pushed a button on his phone.

"Langley, I hear you." It was Keene, his voice tight as it echoed around the room. "We're already scrambling the teams. Everyone is gearing up as we speak, but we don't have the green light yet. We need the last suppliers to meet with their providers, and we need those drugs to seal this case."

Langley dropped his hands and his shoulders slumped. "Unless she has the wire on her, we're blind if they leave that house, Keene. We'll lose both of them."

"I've got cars nearby and one is assigned to Frank. I have agents set to raid the house. I'm monitoring the rest of the shit-storm that's breaking out throughout the ranks. If all hell breaks loose, we'll initiate without the drugs, but not unless I say so." There was a great deal of scuffling on the other end as people talked in the background. "Miller, you three pursue Frank but don't confront him yet. We think he's headed to meet with Rick but we don't know where since they've now stripped their phones and dumped the wire."

"LT, they're leaving in Jenna's car." Carlson announced.

"I have to deal with Red and Greer and make sure nobody gets away," Keene said quickly. "Harris' team is assigned to Rick, coordinate with them." Then he hung up.

Langley threw on his vest while Carlson synchronized

his phone to Frank's microphone through Barnes' transmitter. Miller threw papers in a folder and they hastily piled into the SUV, Langley behind the wheel as Miller dialed his phone.

Carlson grimaced as Langley made a hard right onto the main road, heading towards Frank's house. "Hey, I'm still picking them up but they're in the car driving."

"Barnes!" Miller barked into his phone. "The wire is now in the Datsun, so we need you within three hundred feet of that car to keep transmitting the mic." Miller hung up and turned toward Langley. "Damn, how the hell did she grab it that fast?" Miller shook his head, brow furrowed.

Langley briefly eyed him sideways, then snapped back to focus on his erratic driving. Miller whistled appreciatively while looking at his lap; in it were two radios, a cell phone and his pile of paperwork which he was juggling expertly as Langley skidded around corners and swerved between cars.

Langley glimpsed into the rearview mirror and saw Carlson holding headphones to his ear, the cord that connected to his phone whipping him in the face as Langley turned again to avoid an approaching red light.

Anxious, Langley couldn't stop himself. "What are they saying?"

Carlson shook his head. "Frank dismantled and tossed both their phones in fear of wiretaps. Jenna's asking questions but he won't answer."

Miller was on the phone again. "Harris, what's your 20?" One of the radios bleeped loudly as Miller clapped his other hand over his hear. "What's the plan?"

"Jenna said...wait, they're passing Ninth Street." Carlson said hurriedly.

Langley nodded and swerved to pass a slower car.

Carlson leaned forward, hands still covering his earphones as he looked into the rearview mirror with big eyes. "Frank is scared he's being followed. She's dropping some hints on locations they're passing."

"Jesus." Langley's voice cracked and he gripped the steering wheel, his knuckles white.

"Barnes!" Miller barked again. "Call and coordinate with Harris. They lost GPS since the phones are gone and they don't know where to go, but be careful. Frank is looking for tails."

"Sounds like they're passing the dairies, heading towards the orchards? Or some kind of farm?"

"Where the hell are they going?" Langley mused to himself as they hit the outskirts of the city.

"Safe house?" Miller shrugged with a glance at Langley.

"Uh, I'm losing reception. Last I heard was something about circles and gas."

"They've never been over here before." Miller glowered at his paperwork.

"As far as we know," Langley slammed a hand on the wheel as a hay truck pulled out in front of him.

"Barnes," Miller looked down into his lap. "He's circling back to see if anyone is following him." Miller listened to Barnes a moment before he hung up and looked at Langley. "Barnes said the Feds are tailing Frank and for us to back off so we don't spook him."

"I lost them." Carlson shook his head.

"Why can't we just arrest him? There's enough evidence." Langley interjected. "It'd be safer to do it now."

Miller shook his head as he hung up his phone. "At least one of these guys is hiding the payload or a portion of it. Since the deal is off now that everyone is spooked, we need those drugs otherwise all we have is brief conversations, small-time charges and a lot of hearsay. Not enough to take everyone down without long court battles we might lose."

"What makes you think they're going to get the drugs now?" Langley kept watching oncoming traffic as he idled at the red light.

"What's the first thing everyone does when they're scared?" Miller asked. "They check what's most important. At least one of these idiots will head straight for a hidden stash, and we only need one to close this out. Where do you *think* Frank is going right now, scared shitless as he is while keeping a tight leash on Jenna?"

Just then, Langley saw Jenna's Datsun zoom by in the opposite direction. He only caught a glimpse of a ponytail in the backseat, but it was enough to make his heart leap into his throat.

Langley pulled into the parking lot of the gas station on the edge of town, his legs shaking as he imagined what his team and Jenna would have to go through before the night was over. Miller was staring at his phone, reading something.

"Neil said that Red and his boss are spooked. They're searching everyone for wires and taking phones. Thank God I didn't give him a mic, but he still has to ditch his phone which means he's going dark until we catch up to him or he can find a way out."

"Who's he with?"

Miller shrugged, an exasperated look on his face. "Keene's running him. I don't know the location of Greer or Neil, but hopefully he ends up with Frank and your girl."

Langley mumbled a curse as Miller shook his head.

"You said farms, right Carlson?"

"Jenna said something about missing the old family farm and something about almond trees." Carlson removed one headphone and looked at Langley and Miller in turn.

"How did she slip that into a conversation?" Langley sighed. "He'll have to drive close by here to get to any farms."

Miller nodded. "Stay put. Harris saw Rick get into a car and he's maneuvering similarly to Frank, but they're tailing him too." Miller grabbed a radio. "Boy-64, No, do *not* call air support over east district right now." He shook his head after setting the radio back down. "Last thing we need is a helicopter hovering overhead while we're trying to be stealthy."

Langley's stomach was churning; he suddenly recognized that the operation itself had taken a backseat to Jenna's safety in his mind, and the realization made him swallow hard. *Focus, dammit! The op's success leads to her safety, not the other way around.*

"Barnes!" Miller barked again. "Since we can't tail right now, go out further, find an almond orchard and then park the car somewhere off road so passersby won't see you. Look for a farm while you're at it, your guess is as good as mine. Keep that mic base on." He slammed the phone down with a shrug. "Worth a shot."

Langley wiped his hands on his pants. He could feel beads of sweat forming beneath his tactical vest.

"Who is this?" Miller asked, answering his phone again. "Ok, yeah. *What?!* You *lost him?*"

Langley fired up the engine with a curse.

"Are you *kidding* me right now?" Miller railed. "Keep driving. We'll start looking." Miller added a colorful description of how he felt about the Feds right after hanging up.

Panic took over Langley as he realized that Jenna was now completely alone. There was nothing he could do but drive around and hope that they could find the Datsun somewhere in the city.

CHAPTER TWENTY FOUR

JENNA WAS TREMBLING. The sun was barely casting a glow now, and Frank was maneuvering as if he were in a combat zone: swerve here, erratic turn there, flying through alleys while his eyes constantly scanned everything. Frank was pissed; his jaw was clenched and his face was dark red as he snarled at the mirrors. Jenna could only hope that the microphone was actually working and that someone was listening on the other end, but she had no idea if that was actually the case.

As they maneuvered through the backstreets of the city, Frank began to sweat profusely and had to keep mopping his brow with a dusty sleeve. His eyes became wide and crazed; if Jenna thought she was nervous, her brother was now putting her to shame.

She debated whether attempting an escape would do her any good; the likelihood of her making it over the seat and out the passenger door without Frank grabbing her were slim, and such a move would just create chaos.

Frank mumbled something under his breath as he cut across the last intersection before heading out onto the desolate roads leading to the old cement plant and other nearly-abandoned construction sites. Jenna frowned.

"Frank," Jenna said cautiously, her voice trembling. "Please. Talk to me. What's going on?"

Darkness had taken over the city, but Frank did not turn on the headlights. Instead he cut slowly through a dirt path between some old construction rubble, heading toward the outskirts of the dairy farms.

Frank regarded her emotionlessly through the rearview mirror, but continued to slowly inch the car forward. Jenna wasn't sure what was going on, but Frank looked as if he were scared he might not see the sun rise.

After a long pause filled only with Frank's erratic breathing and noisy sweat-wiping, Frank drove through the middle of a dense bought of trees until Jenna feared they were totally lost inside a maze of dark branches.

"Jenna," he swallowed hard as the car slowed even more. Jenna barely felt the car stop moving and only realized it had when Frank threw it in park and turned his entire body in one swift movement. His hands clutched the headrest as he leaned over the seat, the sweat dripping off his nose onto Jenna's jeans.

Frank panted before speaking again. "This is your chance to come clean to me before anything else happens."

"What?" Jenna's voice was barely audible.

"Tell me the truth." The whites of his eyes glimmered in the scant moonlight.

"Frank, I don't have any idea—"

"Look," he barked, swiping his forehead. "Don't make me regret this. I know you didn't have a one-night-stand with some random drug addict." He growled, spittle flying from his lips.

Jenna couldn't help the almost imperceptible gasp that escaped her lips. She immediately slammed her mouth shut, but Frank pressed on.

"I'm in deep shit and I *need* to know, Jenna." his voice cracked and he sniffed, rubbing a sleeve under his nose. "I screwed up, and I can't protect you anymore."

Jenna slowly turned her head but kept her eyes on her brother's crazed expression. "Frank," she said quietly. "What have you done?"

He turned in the seat and rubbed his hands over his eyes. "If I tell you the truth, you have to tell me the truth. Agreed?"

Jenna nodded, seeing fear mirrored in Frank's eyes.

"I got in too deep. What should have been a simple job for a couple days has turned into a living nightmare."

"What job?"

Frank regarded Jenna again as he dropped his hands onto the seat with a slap. "Storing and moving a lot of drugs."

Jenna crossed her arms over her chest. "Is this a trick? Why the sudden confessions? You acted like you were going to shoot me in your garage." Jenna was incredulous.

"We're all fucked and I'm realizing that I don't want to spend my life running. I'm hoping that Rick was right and that you *are* actually wearing a wire right now."

Jenna's breath caught in her throat and a whole-body shiver took over her, causing her hands to clench her arms involuntarily. "How did you—he—what—"

"I don't want to die tonight. And I never wanted you involved in the first place. Why the hell do you think I told you to stay away from the cops?"

"I didn't ask to be put in the middle of this!"

"But you wired yourself for them? For what purpose!"

"How—how do you know that?"

Frank's laugh was high pitched. "Cops ain't the only

ones that know shit, Jenna. Now hand over the wire."

Jenna felt detached from herself as she dug in her pants and ripped free the sticky microphone.

"Is it on?"

"I have no idea, Frank." Frank held out his hand and Jenna passed it over. "I want you to know that I never meant to betray you." she briefly touched his sweaty palm before he looked the wire over.

Frank's lips were thin, nostrils flared. "Was that druggie you fucked a cop?"

Jenna nodded as Frank rubbed his face. "He's not just some cop, Frank. He is—well, the only man..." Jenna shook her head vigorously. "I have ever...Frank, I love him."

Frank frowned skeptically. "Awfully strong words."

"He tried to keep me out of all this."

"And how's that working out for you?" Frank snorted. Jenna stayed silent as Frank spun the wire between his fingers. "Rick was going to search you when we got there, and they would have found this. I don't know what they would have done to us if they had. I kept telling him you wouldn't do that to me. Looks like I'm the fool." Frank shuffled around in the front seat with the microphone, but Jenna couldn't see what he was doing. He grunted before speaking again. "Jenna, if you deny ever being involved and deny knowing anything about drugs or wires, Rick will lose all credibility. It will shake everyone up and no one will ever think that *I'm* the one wired. What kind of deal you think your cop boyfriend would cut me if I wear this instead of you?"

Jenna couldn't fully comprehend the scenario that Frank had just rattled off; she was still reeling from the abrupt come-to-Jesus moment they were having, and it was getting to be overwhelming.

"Frank, I don't even know if it's on. For all I know it died a long time ago and all of this would be for nothing."

"It's all we have. If they found you with the wire—"

"Why not throw it out the window to save us both?" Jenna mused.

Frank shook his head, sending sweat flying around the car. "Bad idea. We both need all the help we can get right now."

"And why couldn't you have thought of this *before* we left the house? All we would have had to do was make one phone call and none of this would be happening."

Frank held his hands up and shook them. "I can't change the past! I've made a lot of stupid mistakes, alright?" He scratched at his blonde hair with clawed hands. "At least we're doing this now. From this point, all I can do is try to control our future."

Jenna reached her arm forward and put a hand on Frank's shoulder.

"I understand, Frank." She said as he took a deep breath and looked into her eyes. "I'm with you."

Frank put his hand over hers and gave it a hard pat. He managed a weak smile. "I thought Rick was wrong about you. For once, I'm glad *I* was wrong. Glad I stopped to ask you right now. Shit."

As he released her hand, Jenna leaned back and smirked. "Well, looks like I was wrong about you, too."

Frank wiped his nose again and looked at his sister. "What do you mean?"

"I thought you hated cops."

"Oh, I do." Frank barked as he put the car in drive again. "But that doesn't mean we *both* don't need them right now." He continued his slow creep through the darkness. "Pray this shit works, Jenna. I hope your pig friends are listening and that they save us in the end. Don't blow it, Jenna, because the consequences could be deadly."

CHAPTER TWENTY FIVE

LANGLEY SNARLED IN FRUSTRATION, slamming his palms against the side of the SUV. The night was black; there was barely a sliver of moon in the sky and he was shaking with rage at being metaphorically handcuffed to protocol, as well as his apparently incompetent Federal teammates.

Not only had they lost Jenna and Frank, but now they'd lost Rick, too. Other bikers and dealers had scrambled into the woodworks while a few were quietly caught before skipping town. No drugs had turned up yet and everyone was on edge. Langley knew that they had only hours before all hell would break loose and everyone would be gone.

Including Jenna. And who the hell knew what was happening with her right now. Langley tried not to let his imagination get the best of him, but he knew what happened to informants and cop-sympathizers when caught by the gang.

Parked in the lot of a closed restaurant, Miller was screaming at someone on a cell phone while Carlson was still sitting in the back seat of the SUV. Langley leaned on the door frame and looked at Carlson, his teeth grinding together.

"You look shook up," Carlson regarded Langley nervously.

"You think?" Langley couldn't stop himself; he punched the SUV hard, leaving a dent in the door above the handle and a shock of pain through his fist which felt alarmingly satisfying. The action caused Carlson to cringe in his seat. Langley gripped the frame once again with both hands, talking through clenched teeth. "She's the only woman I've—ever—"

"Cared about?" Carlson offered, followed by an audible gulp.

Langley lowered his chin, eyes narrowed. "Yes."

"There are over fifty agents working on this. We'll find Frank and Jenna."

Sighing, Langley cocked his head at Carlson. "Thanks for lying to me, I need that right now."

But Carlson had turned away from him, his face regarding the cell phone he'd been messing with since they lost the microphone's signal. Carlson grappled with the headphones and pressed them to his ears.

"I'm getting static."

"Is that a good thing?" Langley felt a surge of adrenaline course through him.

"It means they're close to Barnes, but not close enough to transmit."

"MILLER!" Langley shouted so loudly that Miller reacted by immediately taking up a defensive position in the middle of the parking lot with his pistol half out of its holster before recovering and running back to the car. "Call Barnes!"

They all piled into the SUV while Langley rolled up the windows from his perch at the driver's seat. Miller hung up and dialed Barnes on speaker, who answered after the first ring.

"About time," she mumbled.

"We're picking up static which means they're close, but we need you closer." Carlson said quickly, leaning forward from the backseat.

"Start moving around. Get out of the car and start jogging with that damn beacon in some direction until we tell you to do something else." Miller clarified.

"Oookay." They heard shuffling and a car door quietly close. They could only hear Barnes steady breathing; Miller and Langley were transfixed on Carlson's face as he focused on the headphones.

"No, I lost the static."

"Go the opposite direction."

Barnes quietly acknowledged.

"Better, sort of."

"Try going right or left." Miller ordered.

Carlson started nodding vigorously.

"Keep going that way, it's working."

Langley held his breath as he stared at Carlson. Agonizing seconds ticked by while Barnes breathed heavily into the phone.

"It's still garbled."

"Keep moving."

Another thirty seconds went by while Barnes jogged, huffing rhythmically.

"Well?" Barnes whispered.

"Still can't make out what they're saying. Too much interference?"

Langley groaned, rubbing his face with his hands.

They heard odd scratching noises through Miller's phone.

"Hey, whatever you're doing is working!" Carlson said excitedly.

"Great," they could barely hear Barnes as she grumbled into the phone. "I'm climbing into a goddamn tree."

Carlson unplugged the headphones; Miller and Langley breathed quietly as they all three leaned towards Carlson. Langley could feel the intense heat of the cell phone as he listened, his legs quivering with anticipation.

"*—shoot me in your garage.*"

Langley felt a shock of giddiness hit him as he heard Jenna's voice.

"*We're all fucked—don't—my life running*" Frank was saying. "*—Rick was—you are actually wearing a wire—*"

"Shit," Miller whispered. "Keep listening and fill me in, I need to brief Keene." Miller slipped out of the SUV as Langley held his breath. Carlson pushed a few buttons on his phone.

"Making sure it's recording," he said quietly. Langley put a finger to his lips angrily.

"*—cops ain't the—ones that know shit, Jenna. –hand over the wire. –on?*"

Miller hopped back into the car and quickly shut the door.

"*—meant to betray you.*" Jenna was saying. Miller held his phone close to Carlson's without saying a word.

"*—that druggie you fucked a cop?*" Both Carlson and Miller looked at Langley with wide eyes. Langley's teeth clamped together as they all held their breath.

"*—not just some cop—well, the only—I have—Frank, I love him.*"

"Ho!" Miller hooted, a hand flying to his mouth.

Langley abruptly choked on his own saliva and quickly retreated to his seat, his ears hot as he coughed. Miller's cheeks were red as he tried to smother his snorting. Langley maintained a distance from Carlson's phone, head buried in his hand as he tried to take a steadying breath, barely hearing Frank.

"*—working out for you?*" Frank was saying. "*—search you—would have found this. I don't—what they would—done to us if they had. I kept—you wouldn't do that—I'm the—Jenna—deny ever being involved—drugs and wires, Rick will—credibility. No one—dream that I'm the one wired. What kind of deal—cop boyfriend would cut—I wear this instead of you?*"

"Holy hell." Miller jumped back out of the car with his phone and slammed the door.

"*—know it died a long time ago—be for nothing.*" Jenna was saying, her tone ominous. Langley's heart was in his throat and he coughed again, feeling as if he were suddenly drowning.

The door opened again and Miller hopped in for a third time. Langley felt like part of a circus act as Miller shut the door again. "Let's roll. Harris' team will meet us at Barnes' location."

Langley fired up the car as Carlson plugged the headphones back in, denying Langley the comfort of hearing Jenna's voice. *Just hang on, Jenna. We're coming.*

CHAPTER TWENTY SIX

JENNA TOOK COMFORT IN knowing that her brother was doing his best to rectify his mistakes; she, however, was in full support of running the other way and letting it all play out without them being involved, but Frank was adamant that they go in. Trying to trap Rick—verbally for the cops listening through the wire or physically if necessary—was Frank's only hope of redemption and a reduced sentence. Jenna was trying not to panic; her brother's sudden confidence wasn't enough to make her feel any better, although she was certainly grateful they both now knew each others' truths.

As Frank approached the barn that he'd hurriedly told her about as they drove, he hit the headlights.

"Remember, I'm not on your side." Frank shook his head with gritted teeth. He had stopped sweating and seemed to have regained his bearings. Jenna was still terrified and let it take over her as she began to squirm in the backseat, creating a visual of her fighting to get out.

With a sharp spin of the wheel, Frank skidded into the barn and the barn doors were quickly slammed shut. The car doors were yanked open by two men Jenna had never seen before; Frank leapt out and Jenna recoiled in the backseat.

"What are you—" Jenna shrieked, but a beefy hand clapped over her mouth as she was yanked from the car. Another solid arm wrapped around her and she lashed out, kicking and connecting with shins, knees and anything else she could. Her crazed fighting managed to send both her and her captor crumpling to the ground, but a second man jumped in and ratcheted her arms behind her. With a last shriek, Jenna felt herself lifted off the ground and her shoulder's strained from the torque.

"Get off me!" Jenna screamed before Rick lunged toward her and slapped a strip of duct tape over her mouth.

Dust swirled around the dimly lit barn as Jenna continued to struggle. Rick stood, waiting patiently. After another minute, Jenna was exhausted and ceased her futile attacks; both her arms and legs were wrapped up by the immensely muscled man that was holding her, the back of Jenna's head barely reaching his sternum.

With a nod from Rick, a man came to stand before Jenna with a crooked, lewd smile. As her captor clamped her arms harder, the man in front of her grabbed her shoulders gruffly, then slid them over her breasts with a rough squeeze.

Jenna bucked and squirmed, but the hands were unwavering. Instead of groping her again, the vulgar man methodically swept his hands through her sweater. It was lifted over her head as all the men in the barn cat-called and whistled; filthy hands traced the wire of her bra and Jenna snarled against the duct tape.

Her sweater was pulled back down and he reached for the button of her pants. She felt her captor's grip on her legs loosen; Jenna wriggled a leg free and slammed her knee into the groper's groin, causing him to double over with a grunt.

Jenna felt herself sailing backwards before being strategically slammed to the ground. One man pinned her arms above her head while two more grabbed her legs. Thrashing, Jenna saw Frank standing off to one side, his arms crossed over his chest as he calmly watched.

Rick had taken over the assault and was swiftly unbuttoning Jenna's jeans. He plunged his hand into her pants and fished around, running his hand along her lacy underwear as Jenna fought with everything she had left.

"Strip her." Rick barked, motioning to two other men.

Jenna squealed against the duct tape as her clothes were abruptly ripped from her body.

As the last of her dignity and clothing was stripped away, Jenna was released and discarded on the cold wooden floor as they focused on scrutinizing her clothes, nothing upon her body but the strip of duct tape covering her mouth. She hugged her knees to her chest and stayed sitting as the tall, brutish man that had held her captive took a knee beside her. Jenna snarled against the duct tape, tears of anger tickling her cheeks but the man made no move toward her. He just regarded the other men in the barn with a face of placidity. It was apparent he knew Jenna wouldn't be attempting to leave; he didn't even bother to restrain her as she sat shivering on the ground.

All the men, aside from her brother, Rick and the two men scrutinizing her clothes and shoes, were lewdly fondling themselves and making snide comments. One man approached Jenna and the man kneeling beside her cursed violently and flexed his arms, causing the assaulter to stumble backwards; Jenna felt unexpectedly comforted by the action and watched the veins on the man's neck twitch as he glared at the other men in the barn, almost daring them all to try and come near her again. *Thank God at least one of them has some semblance of honor.*

"There's nothing here, Rick." One of the men tossed Jenna's bra behind him in exasperation.

"There has to be." Rick's brow furrowed and he immediately tore at one of Jenna's shoes.

"Unless it's one of these damn buttons, there's no wire here." The other man exclaimed.

Her captor suddenly got to his feet. Jenna nervously watched him as he walked away from her, afraid someone might try something in his absence; his broad back flexed as he bent and retrieved all of Jenna's clothes from the dirty barn floor. The men searching her clothes looked towards him but chose to stay silent as he regarded them sharply.

Jenna clutched her knees tighter, her arms shaking violently. She was too afraid to touch the duct tape in fear the consequences would be much worse. The tall, muscular man returned and knelt in front of her, his eyes never wavering from her face as he set the clothes at Jenna's feet. He pointed a finger at her as Jenna blinked away tears, gesturing towards the duct tape.

"I'll take it off if you promise not to make a sound—*any* sound at all. Agreed?" His deep voice was steady, commanding.

Jenna nodded her head as she lifted her chin. With one quick yank he tore the strip off with a loud *rip*.

"Put your clothes on." He murmured, standing in front of her and blocking the view for the crude bikers as she started hastily pulling on her underclothes. When she finally pulled her sweater over her trembling arms, the man moved to stand behind her.

Rick had begun arguing with Frank and two other men; they'd moved their conversation to a corner of the barn and

Jenna couldn't make out any of what they were saying. There seemed to be general dissention as Frank had predicted; there were twelve men inside the barn and all of them—now no longer distracted by a naked woman—seemed to coming to terms with a fearful reality and all of them were discussing it amongst themselves.

"Jenna."

The whisper was so faint Jenna thought it might be her imagination, but she turned slightly towards the sound; the brawny man that had held her captive was scanning the barn with his eyes but his body leaned towards her.

He sneered as he stepped towards her, his eyes still focused on the men in the barn. He roughly grabbed her arm, pulling her into a weak arm lock as he whispered in her ear. "Your *Langley's* Jenna?"

"Yes!" Jenna hissed. She barely contained a sob. Just hearing David's name amidst the trauma made her knees weak as she realized she wasn't alone.

Frank and Rick were wrapping up their discussion and Jenna took the last moment she might have to fill in the man—*cop?*—before she might not have another chance.

Careening her neck around as if she were fighting the hold, she quickly mumbled towards the man's ear. "Frank has the wire."

He blinked acknowledgement and then shoved her forward by a shoulder as the men gathered together.

"She's coming with us. I don't trust her." Rick scowled.

Jenna glowered at Rick, but stayed silent.

"You know what to do. Get moving." Rick snarled at the men and everyone immediately headed towards the back door as Frank turned off the lights.

Plunged into darkness, Jenna felt the hold on her loosen before she felt the man squeeze one of her hands reassuringly.

"I've got you." He whispered.

Jenna could only barely make out figures as they tromped blindly through dirt, brush and gravel in silence, only the sounds of rhythmic breathing disturbing the night ambience. She didn't even realize they had reached another outlying building until she was shoved inside another set of open doors.

Once the doors were closed behind her, someone switched on a dim lantern.

Jenna blinked against the sudden brightness. She quickly scanned the inside of the converted horse barn as men shuffled quietly in and out of the shadows. The row of strange-looking motorcycles were the most noteworthy; Jenna also noticed a heap of discarded blankets and some tattered old horse equipment strewn around stacks of old construction lumber. Jenna frowned, trying to ascertain what Rick and the men had planned.

But her eyes were quickly covered by a thin cloth and her hands were bound together roughly behind her back by a second man with icy hands. Jenna bit her lip surreptitiously as she realized the man was wrapping her wrists with what seemed to be an entire roll of duct tape. The cloth that was now tied around her eyes was semi-transparent; Jenna assumed that her bodyguard had arranged it that way so that she could manage to see through it and she breathed a small sigh of relief, grateful for the small advantage.

Jenna was grabbed by the shoulders and shoved into something, her back scraping against a wall of splinters.

"Be still, and be silent." Someone hissed in her ear. She gave one nod of her head to acknowledge the command.

As the figure retreated, Jenna slowly canted her head to try and make out shapes. She could distinguish Rick, who was whispering with a few other men close to the lantern which now hung on a wall. Frank was standing off to the side, closest to the motorcycles. He approached Rick but was stopped by a gruff wave of Rick's hand.

Jenna held her breath. *I hope the cops are close.* She shivered as a sense of dread washed over her. *What if they don't even know we're here?*

Suddenly, Jenna battled with an overwhelming urge to sneeze as she caught a whiff of something extremely spicy. Another lantern was lit and Jenna could make out the shapes of the motorcycles and a pile of something that some of the men were digging through and putting on their bodies. Two men were loading what appeared to be boxes into the cargo carriers of the bikes.

Someone had donned a helmet and backpack, and then sat on one of the bikes. With a nod, the back barn door was opened and the bike surged forward without any sound; as the bike reached the barn doors, the only noise it emitted was a high-pitched whirr, the likes of which Jenna had never heard before.

Another bike followed close behind, but before a third could make it out the door Frank confronted Rick, their argument going from quiet to shouting within moments.

"—leave me *hanging!*" Frank screeched.

There was cursing and a scuffle broke out. Jenna couldn't make out individuals amidst the commotion, but she heard Frank swear as a punch landed solidly on someone. Another fight broke out simultaneously near the line of motorcycles and she could no longer discern anything amidst the dust and general pandemonium.

Knowing she was at least momentarily forgotten, Jenna

swiftly took action; she separated her feet and straightened her arms behind her back so that her wrists were parallel inside the duct tape. She froze a moment, suspended, her breath shallow as she felt adrenaline begin to flow through her.

"Burn, you idiot!" Rick sneered. More bikes surged from the barn, swerving around the brawling men to escape.

As Jenna heard the metallic rack of a pistol slide, she flexed her shoulder muscles and wrenched her arms in a scissoring motion, splitting the tape clean in half and instantly freeing her hands.

"*Help!*" Frank screamed.

Tearing the shoddy blindfold off while discarding the stream of tape, Jenna could now clearly see the glimmer of a pistol in Rick's hands. Her bodyguard was wrapped up with three other men who were wielding pieces of lumber like clubs; Frank was on his knee, panting and too far away to react if Rick decided to pull the trigger.

Jenna charged towards Rick, the general chaos of the tussle with the bikes covering the sound of her shoes on the wood. She dove, her outstretched hands ramming solidly into Rick's; the gun bounced wildly inside his grip as Jenna collided with him and sent him stumbling sideways.

"Bitch!" He roared, muscling Jenna with one hand, his other gripping the pistol with a finger teasing the trigger.

"*Freeze!* Drop the gun, drop the gun!"

Jenna shrieked as Rick slammed the butt of the pistol into her clavicle.

"Carlson, help Neil!"

"Drop the gun!"

Jenna tried to dive out of the way, knowing that a hail of bullets was certain to rain down upon her and Rick at any moment. But her momentum was stopped when a knee caught her in the stomach and a powerful arm wrapped around her neck.

"Don't shoot her!" Frank screamed.

Jenna closed her eyes in defeat; she realized that saving her brother might come at the cost of her own life. The cold muzzle of the pistol grazed her cheek as she clutched the forearm that was crushing her throat.

"Fuck!" There was a crash of motorcycles and bodies, followed by the clicks of handcuffs.

"No! *Jenna!*"

Tears sprang to Jenna's eyes as she heard David yell. Jenna could feel the anguish in his voice as he cried out her name; she couldn't see him amidst the chaos of shadowy bodies, but knowing he was there was enough to light a fire within her, one that screamed for her to fight back with everything she had.

"Harris, get him!" Someone shouted.

Struggling to breath, Jenna gritted her teeth and pushed off the ground as hard as she could, bringing a knee up high. On the way down she drove her foot back and connected solidly with Rick's shin.

As Rick howled in pain, Jenna shoved Rick's elbow upward with both hands and dropped her body weight, wriggling out of the choke hold. Rick groped at her shoulder and she squirmed in his arms, spinning her body to twist out of his grasp. She heard David's panicked cry once more as she pushed off of Rick's broad chest.

"Jenna!"

The night exploded before her eyes.

CHAPTER TWENTY SEVEN

LANGLEY FINALLY DISLODGED the knife from the biker's hands with a powerful twist of his wrist, sending him sprawling backwards with Langley following him down to the ground.

"Don't shoot her!" He heard Jenna's brother scream as he struggled to get the handcuffs on the cursing, flailing biker.

"Fuck!" Miller shouted as he and Neil were ambushed by two more club-wielding bikers, sending them crashing into the row of remaining motorcycles. Langley hastily snapped the cuffs on the biker and looked frantically around the badly lit barn.

Then Langley identified the cause of Frank's shout; Rick had an arm clamped over Jenna's throat and was clutching a pistol in his other hand, muzzling Jenna's face.

"No! *Jenna!*" Langley screamed as he abandoned the cuffed biker.

"Harris, get him!" Neil yelled, pointing to a man sprinting out of the barn.

As Harris bolted out the barn door, Langley jumped over the pile of motorcycles and people while he heard Rick yowl in pain.

When Langley saw Jenna break free of Rick's grasp, he had enough time to scream once more, knowing that nothing he could do would stop Rick in time.

"Jenna!" He shrieked, fluidly drawing his sidearm as he ran.

Rick pulled the trigger, muzzle flash illuminating the barn and the crack of the pistol deafening everyone in the room.

Jenna fell away from Rick and hit the ground on her side, sliding across the dusty barn floor.

Langley fired twice, hitting Rick in the hip and high in the shoulder. The smell of burnt powder ignited the wrath within him and he screamed his frustration; the ten feet remaining between him and Jenna felt like miles.

Frank stumbled to his feet and jumped over Jenna to tackle Rick, who was bellowing and clutching his shoulder as the pistol hung loose at his side. Miller was close behind and collided with the other two men, sending all of them to the ground. Langley covered the distance to Jenna and slid onto his knees as he holstered his pistol, immediately scooping her into his arms.

"Jesus," Langley fought against the stinging tears in his eyes, feeling stickiness in her hair. Her whole body trembled against his as he tried to determine where the blood was coming from.

"Lang!" Miller shouted.

Langley twisted himself, shielding Jenna with his body as another round was fired; Langley felt a blast of heat and grunted against the feeling of a hundred hot needles hitting his arm and face. His ears rang intensely as he saw Miller and Frank tangled with Rick, the pistol finally skittering toward the barn door.

The barn was abruptly bathed in light as someone lit a bright lantern.

Hands shaking, Langley grabbed Jenna's shoulders and sat her upright. He sat hard onto the heels of his boots with his knees straddling Jenna's lithe frame. Langley heard handcuffs click and glanced over to see Rick still writhing on the ground underneath Frank and Miller.

Jenna's eyes opened wide and she sucked in air as she grabbed Langley's flexed forearms, digging her nails into his skin. Langley looked at the black, sooty smudge and pronounced stippling that smattered her right cheek. He placed a hand on each side of her head and she recoiled with a grimace.

"Are you okay?" Langley saw his left hand was covered in blood; Jenna cupped her ear and squeezed her eyes shut. A streak of blood had streamed down her neck and onto her sweater. Vision blurred, Langley wiped the sweat, blood and tears from his stinging eyes with his sleeve. When he could see clearly again, he saw Jenna's bright blue eyes were staring hard at his face.

"I am now."

Still sitting on his knees, Langley circled his arms around her and pulled her to his chest. She clutched the back of his vest and pressed herself against him, her breath coming in short gasps.

Langley rested his cheek on her head, squeezing his eyes shut. He took a deep breath and grasped her tighter as they trembled in each others' arms.

After a time, Langley opened his eyes and saw that Frank was standing behind Jenna, his hands loose at his sides. As the two men's gazes met, Frank gave a curt nod before speaking.

"Is she okay?" He asked, his voice cracking.

Langley felt Jenna relax and responded by releasing her from their embrace. Frank offered a hand to Langley; Langley took it and Frank pulled him to his feet. They both grabbed Jenna and carefully stood her upright between them; Rick yowled in the background as he and the other bikers were dragged outside the barn.

"I'm alright," Jenna said as she tenderly traced her fingers along her cheek and ear. Wincing, she turned towards her brother.

"It should've been me, not you." Frank grabbed his sister into a tight hug. "You saved my life."

As they embraced one another, Miller came to stand beside Langley.

All three of them regarded Miller when he cleared his throat, a pair of handcuffs loose in his hand.

"Frank," Miller said respectfully. "We've been listening since you took the wire in the orchard. What you did was noble, and you helped all of us—" Miller gestured to Langley with an open hand, "when you tackled Rick and helped me subdue him. All of this will certainly help your case. But, I regret that I still have to..."

"I get it." Frank nodded as he released Jenna, who quickly slid into Langley's waiting arms. "I'm just hoping it will make a difference, you know, in the end."

"It will." Miller affirmed.

"I'd testify on your behalf." Langley said without hesitation, rubbing his hand lightly over Jenna's shivering shoulder as she wove her arms around his waist, squeezing him tightly.

"I would too." Neil interjected, rubbing his neck as he strolled over to stand beside Langley.

"Thanks." Frank said, biting one side of his lip as he nodded his head.

Langley extended his hand and Frank slowly took it, the two men shaking once before mutually releasing.

Frank pointed at Langley's face, then touched his own lip briefly. "Sorry about that."

Langley shrugged his shoulders. "You were only trying to protect your sister," he patted Jenna's shoulder affectionately.

Frank snorted, shaking his head. "Funny the way that worked out." With a sigh, Frank turned around and allowed Miller to handcuff him.

"I'll take him to Keene." Neil offered. Miller nodded once.

"Thank you, Neil. For everything." Jenna reached her hand out and grabbed the big cop's arm.

Neil stopped and somberly regarded Jenna as he covered her hand with his own. His eyes flicked to Langley before he spoke. "I'm sorry I didn't stop them."

Jenna shook her head, swallowing hard. Langley tensed, frowning at Neil with the intent to ask what he was talking about, but Jenna's hand pressed into his stomach underneath his vest, making him inhale sharply.

"We might not be here if you had." She sniffed while idly rubbing her fingers along Langley's torso in a smooth motion. Langley felt himself take a deep breath, her touch calming his agitation.

Neil released Jenna and put his hand briefly on Langley's shoulder. With a last glance at Langley and Jenna, Frank and Neil sauntered out of the barn accompanied by the roar of a helicopter passing overhead.

Harris suddenly clapped a hand on Langley's back and Carlson coughed as he came to stand beside Miller.

"Where's Barnes?" Miller looked around the barn.

"She's pursuing the getaway bikes with my team in the

car." Harris let his hand drop. "So, I need a ride out of here."

Miller sighed, dropping his chin to his chest. "Goddamn. We have a lot of work to do." Miller looked at Langley and Jenna. "I need pictures for evidence. Forensics and the FBI suits are almost here, then we're taking you both to the hospital."

Langley frowned, glancing down at his arm. There were at least twenty streaks of blood covering his right arm and he assumed the same marks were on his face, courtesy of Rick's second round ripping through wood and debris, sending shrapnel flying everywhere. Langley could barely feel it given the adrenaline high he was still experiencing.

After teams with cameras and evidence markers began to process the barn, Jenna and Langley were photographed and a few shots were snapped of Carlson and Harris. Langley was taken aside and he somberly handed over his pistol to two men. One of the men grabbed Langley's arm and gave him a heartfelt squeeze of sympathy.

They all exited the barn and met the chill night air. The SUV sat alone in the dark and Langley tossed his head at Carlson while stripping his vest off in one smooth motion.

"You're driving."

Jenna slid into the back seat between David and the man named Harris. In the faint moonlight, she could still see the numerous streaks of still-damp blood covering Langley's face and arm, but he didn't even seem to notice or care.

In all her life, Jenna had never felt safer than being in that car with those four cops; she actually found herself nodding off in the comfort of Langley's powerful, warm arms as they drove despite the throbbing pain in her ear and head, the ringing in her ears finally calming to a dull annoyance.

The hospital rendered immediate treatment and helped Jenna remove the soot and dried blood from her hair, face and neck. Although sore, her collar bone was fortunately only bruised. The bullet, however, had torn through a large portion of her ear; some stitches later, she found Carlson standing outside the door to the ER.

"Hi." He said with a small smile. "You want to sit down or anything?"

"No, thanks." Jenna murmured, clutching her shoulders in the brisk night air.

"Detective Langley's not out yet." Carlson shuffled his feet before leaning against the door of their SUV. He chuckled quietly to himself. "Man, I've never seen him so angry before."

"Who?" Jenna asked, confused.

Carlson pointed a thumb over his shoulder at the door of the SUV. "When they lost track of you and your brother, Detective Langley went a little nuts."

Jenna saw the dent near the door handle and raised an eyebrow at Carlson.

"He heard you, you know."

"What?" Jenna couldn't keep up with Carlson's abrupt changing of the subject.

"Detective Langley. He heard you and Frank talking about him while you were in the orchard. Well, we were all listening in on that conversation." Carlson cleared his throat.

Jenna bit her bottom lip, feeling suddenly warm against the chill air.

"That was nothing in comparison to what we heard—" Carlson abruptly stopped mid-sentence and dropped his arms, gulping as he regarded the look of confusion on Jenna's face. He shifted uncomfortably while watching the doors to the ER swing open. "Forget I said anything." He added hastily.

David stepped out in his jeans and black t-shirt, eyes searching the parking lot for a moment before settling on Carlson and Jenna.

"You okay?" He asked as he strolled over, placing his hands on her arms. But she was prevented from answering by Langley's lips suddenly and firmly pressing against hers. "Sorry. I couldn't stop myself."

"I don't mind." She hugged him briefly before they all climbed into the SUV.

Carlson was at the wheel, but Miller and Harris were gone.

"Where'd they go?" Langley asked.

"Woods was around, gave 'em a ride. Miller said Keene would like to take statements tonight if you each can handle it."

Langley nodded as Jenna sank into his arms once more.

"So, Jenna. I, uh, I think I understand now why Detective Langley is so in—"

"Carlson."

"I'll shut up."

"Thank you."

The drive was silent. But arriving at the police station destroyed the peacefulness when two men immediately approached the car.

"Detective," some FBI agent barked as he swung open the door of the SUV. "IA is waiting for you in room four. Jenna York? Please come with me."

Fear gripped her momentarily and she clung to David's arm as he slid out of the vehicle.

He turned and smiled at her reassuringly, leaning back inside the SUV. "Don't worry, you're not detained," he kissed her forehead softly. "You don't have to do this right now if you don't want to."

"No, I'd rather get it over with while it's still vivid in my mind."

David nodded once, taking her hand in his. "Mine might take awhile."

"I'll be waiting for you." Jenna squeezed his hand. David retreated and turned toward a policeman who handed him a pistol, accompanied by a robust handshake. He and the officer walked away and Jenna followed the FBI agent who watched her intensely.

As she followed a step behind him, he turned to her and smirked, his eyes jovial.

"What?" She asked skeptically.

"Don't worry ma'am, everyone is intimately aware that you are Detective Langley's girl." His smile widened as they entered the doors of the station. "And I'd like to say that you've got a *serious* pair of *cojones*, lady."

CHAPTER TWENTY EIGHT

LANGLEY SUFFERED THROUGH hours of recanting the operation's events. After rehashing every movement and moment to a video camera and what seemed to be a panel of Internal Affairs, FBI and Brookside PD suits that had all gathered in the middle of the night to witness the end of the momentous investigation, they worked the timeline backward and asked numerous questions, ensuring that nothing was missed.

Finishing off the small cup of water set before him, Langley let out a sigh of relief as the cameras were finally switched off and the men in the room exchanged handshakes and congratulations.

"You've had quite the adventure these past few months, Detective." Some older Brookside PD representative nodded his head appreciatively.

Langley grunted acknowledgement as he leaned forward in his chair, not quite trusting his legs enough to stand just yet.

"Detective, would you like for us to provide you someone to talk to regarding what you've been through tonight?"

Before Langley could think of replying, he was cut short by an FBI agent slapping himself on the leg while barking a laugh.

"I'm certain he already has someone specific in mind to *talk* to, Captain."

Langley frowned as a few men in the room chuckled. When a Brookside cop winked at him admiringly, Langley turned to the highest-ranking person he could find. "I'm sorry, but how many people are privy to...that, uh, recording?"

"Sorry, son. Pretty much everyone with a badge in this building has heard it at least once."

"At least...?" Langley groaned as he sank forward, his elbows hitting the table while he buried his head in his hands. "Never mind, I do *not* want to know." He mumbled from the darkness of his arms. There were hearty laughs as equipment was moved and the doors were opened.

"Don't worry, Detective. We're all just in awe of your...capabilities."

"Oh Jesus." Langley sat upright with a look of disgust, covering his eyes with one hand while waving the other before him in surrender. "Don't—please, just stop."

Langley could hear laughter in the hallways and he wasn't certain he could bring himself to leave the room at all.

A young FBI agent put his arms up when he danced past Langley's table, playing an imaginary violin as he giggled childishly.

"It's a *cello*, you idiot." Langley growled moodily, watching him from the gaps between his fingers.

But then Keene was there beside him, pulling Langley to his feet with a firm handshake.

"You local cops don't do too badly under fire, according to Harris' statement."

"It was hell."

"I know." Keene regarded Langley calmly. "You're the last one; I need you for an operational debrief, then I'm moving my team back to my office where the coffee doesn't taste like shit."

Keene led the way, excusing himself and clearing a path for him and Langley.

The debrief lasted longer than Langley expected; he was both exhausted from a hellacious and stressful night while also anxious to find Jenna and get her away from the police station; the last thing he wanted was for someone to make a snide comment about that recording before he could explain the entire situation to her. When the meeting finalized, Langley went to slip quickly out the door, but his arm was grabbed firmly by Miller.

"LT, I just want to—"

"I know, Langley. I wanted to inform you that you are now on a week of administrative leave," Miller ordered, "and I wanted to talk with both you and Jenna before you go."

Langley swallowed and nodded as he exited the conference room. His search only took a moment; Jenna was curled in Carlson's office chair, her head resting on her arm as she took deep, rhythmic breaths. The stitches in her ear were red and swollen and a light stippling pattern was still visible on her cheek, but it was apparent her exhaustion had conquered her pain; Jenna's lips were slightly parted as she slept soundly at the desk.

Langley felt his chest swell with satisfaction as he watched her rest peacefully, realizing that the operation was truly over and that nothing now stood in the way of them going forward. Langley crouched down, lowering himself to one knee so he was close to her as he touched her arm lightly.

"Jenna?"

Her eyes immediately opened and she scanned the room quickly before realization set in.

"Sorry." She righted herself in the chair and shook her head slightly, eyes blinking against the bright lights as Langley rested his arm on her knee.

Miller put a hand on Langley's shoulder and sat on the edge of Carlson's desk, regarding them both as Langley stayed kneeling next to Jenna's chair.

"I already spoke to the team processing your brother's house, Jenna. Detective Langley will escort you and you'll be able to collect your things. And Langley, unfortunately you've got to pack up and move because I don't need Rick trying to call a hit on you from jail since he knows your address."

Langley nodded stoically.

Miller produced a set of keys and handed them to Jenna. "Your car is parked right outside. As for you, Detective," Miller glared fiercely at Langley. "Now that this mess is over and Jenna is safe, you need to promise me that you won't be putting yourself in the path of any more bullets, cars, tasers or fists."

"I promise."

"Good. Jenna? Promise me you'll hold him to that."

"I promise."

"Great. Now get the hell out of here. I don't want to see your ass for a week."

As Langley stood, Miller grabbed Langley into a quick hug. "Take care of yourself. I know I don't need to tell you to take care of her."

Miller sauntered away with a smirk, leaving the two of them at Carlson's desk. Langley offered Jenna a hand and she slowly got to her feet.

"David," Jenna lifted her head as she coiled her hand around his arm. "I don't want to assume anything here, but..."

"Jenna, I'd be delighted if you'd pick somewhere you would like for both of us to move into as soon as possible."

She blinked, then nodded. "Okay, that was easy enough." She shifted uncomfortably, withdrawing her hand.

Langley frowned as he regarded her flushed cheeks and full lips. She seemed to be struggling to say something, but after a moment she pressed her lips together with a sniff, remaining silent.

Langley smiled when she finally looked up to his face. "There's nothing to worry about," he pulled her into a friendly hug and she relaxed in his arms. "After what we've been through, I'm certain we'll get through anything together."

Langley leaned over and nuzzled the top of her head as he began to lead her through a crowd of suits and uniforms towards the door of the station. Langley glared at certain people who were giving him sly thumbs up.

"Alright, that's it." Jenna stopped, releasing Langley with a scowl. "What does everyone know that I don't?"

Langley internally grimaced. "You don't want to know."

Jenna's eyebrows shot up and she tilted her head, eyes narrowing. "Try me."

He reached toward her, but she leaned back. Langley lowered his voice. "I'll tell you in the car."

"No. Tell me now. You just said 'we'll get through anything together.' So start talking."

Groaning, Langley leaned close to Jenna and rested his hands on her shoulders. Her nostrils flared as she glared at him and Langley gritted his teeth, his eyes focused on hers. He did not want to cause a rift between them already; he swallowed hard, not knowing how Jenna was going to handle the truth in the middle of a room full of cops. "Remember that night you came to my apartment and we had sex—twice—in the middle of this investigation?"

Jenna's eyebrows shot up and her jaw dropped open before she whispered angrily. "*Obviously* I remember."

"Well," Langley spread his arms wide, glancing at some of the smirks on his coworker's faces. "Every person in this room heard us, compliments of a wiretap I didn't know was in my apartment."

"Oh my God."

"I told you, you didn't want to know." Langley could hear muffled chuckles coming from some of the cops standing close by. He cleared his throat nervously, watching Jenna for any indication that she might lose it over such an intrusion into her life.

"Is it still there?" She glared, lips pursed.

"No. Well, they told me it wasn't."

"That's too bad," she pouted. Jenna smirked mischievously.

Langley blinked, confused.

With a flip of her hair, she suddenly reached her hand around and loudly slapped Langley's ass, giving it a hard squeeze as she pulled him flush against her.

Langley's mouth dropped as he hurriedly tried to pry Jenna's hands off of his backside, his cheeks suddenly hot. Her hands were unmovable and she smiled wickedly.

The police station became abruptly silent.

Jenna batted her eyelashes. "I was hoping we could give everyone something even *more* exciting to talk about."

ABOUT THE AUTHOR

M. Leann is a former law enforcement officer, defense contractor and stunt woman. After spending her days getting shot at, blown up, beat up and otherwise maimed, M. decided to slow down and enjoy the softer side of life - horseback riding, archery, writing and photography. A California native, M. met and married her own romance hero and is living happily ever after.

You can reach her at MLeann562@gmail.com.

Made in the USA
San Bernardino, CA
22 September 2017